SOUND OF SILENCE

ALI WINTERS

SOUND OF SILENCE

ALI WINTERS

RISING FLAME PRESS

More by Ali Winters

The Hunted series
The Reapers
The Exodus
The Moirai
The Fallen
Flirting with Death

In The End duology
Sound of Silence
Light in Darkness

Shadow World
The Vampire Debt
The Vampire Curse
The Vampire Court
The Vampire Oath
The Vampire Crown
The Vampire Betrayal

Stand Alone
Cast In Moonlight
Favor of the Gods
A Sky of Shattered Stars
Army of the Winter Court

I used to look up at the stars and wonder

if they ever looked back.

- Raylinn Marrow

For Mita,

You are an anchor in a world of chaos.

CHAPTER ONE

The Arrival

Everybody always talked about wanting world peace. But nobody expected to achieve it quite this way…

Silence is everywhere.

Sure, it's peaceful now, but at what cost? It was never in human nature for everyone to get along, but no one thought of that. They just wanted peace, they didn't care how, or what, that meant.

So when *they* came, we got exactly what we asked for.

I still remember exactly where I was that day when the ships landed. It was the beginning and it was the end. The end of my life, the end of the world, the end of reality as I knew it, and at the same time, the beginning of everything new and uncertain.

Nothing would ever be the same again.

The sun had risen, filling the sky with brilliant reds, pinks, and blues, as I stepped out the front door on my first day of spring break of my sophomore year.

My morning run had been nothing out of the ordinary; it was as memorable as every other one.

Quiet.

Most people were still in their beds sleeping, or just waking to the sound of their alarm clocks if they were unlucky enough to have worked that Saturday.

Sweat dripped down my brow as I fell into a rhythm. My feet kept the beat with the pounding of the music in my ears. It wasn't until I was half way through that the sky had darkened.

The second the sun was overshadowed, I turned and headed home, not wanting to get caught in a sudden shower of rain the Northwest was famous for.

Nearing my home, I stopped in my tracks. One of my neighbors, a few blocks away from my house, was standing in his driveway next to his car, just staring upward like he'd been frozen in time. My eyes followed his gaze, and I found exactly what had made him react in such a way.

I had expected a large rain cloud, a plane, a weather balloon, or at worst, the beginning of a funnel forming in the sky. Nothing could have prepared me for the large ship hovering a mile above my head.

It wasn't the saucer-shaped ship you'd expect from decades of watching sci-fi shows and movies, but a flattened, bullet shape, which appeared to be made of one solid piece of seamless metal.

I swallowed hard and turned my gaze to the rest of the sky. Several more hovered miles apart, as if they were forming a large net as far as the eye could see. The moment held me in awe. I wanted to look away… I wanted to run.

But just like my neighbor, the impossible scene above captured my attention completely.

I took a step back and stumbled. My heel caught on the curb and I fell back. The cord of my ear buds caught on my hand and ripped out of my ears with a painful *pop*.

I reached back to catch myself as I landed hard on my butt. My wrist gave out, already throbbing from the impact, causing me to fall to my back and hit my head against the concrete. I wrenched my arm out from under me. The pain brought me out of my trance. Carefully, I flexed the joint. It hurt like hell, but it wasn't broken.

A deafening roar filled the air. With a gravel-crusted palm, I pushed loose strands of sweaty, brown hair out of my eyes. I looked back at the ships in the sky, knowing the sound came from them. Heat radiated off the metal and blew such a fierce wind beneath the ship the air wavered, which made me grateful I was already on the ground.

My heart pounded in my chest as they began lowering. The

thundering of engines grew louder as they fell behind the tree line, then silenced.

It was the silence that seemed the loudest.

By the time they'd all vanished from sight, I was more breathless than any run had ever left me. I almost choked on the air as I struggled to pull it into my lungs.

I scrambled up to my feet and ran home, cutting through the neighbors' yards, not caring as I crushed the prized flowers next door.

Bursting through the door, I yelled out, "Mom! Dad!"

They ran down the stairs, meeting me as I doubled over, once again struggling to breathe.

"Raylinn!" My dad called as he hit the landing, my mom following close behind. Seconds later, he was in front of me, grabbing me by the arms and forcing me to look at him. Dark brown eyes, exactly like mine, filled with worry as they scanned my face. "What happened?"

I looked past him to my mom standing at the bottom of the stairs, eyes wide with her hand over her mouth.

I couldn't help the overwhelming feeling that came over me to want to have my parents wrap their arms around me and make sense of the world like they used to when I was little.

When I turned back to my dad, he was holding me at a distance, looking to see if I'd been hurt.

"Ray, what's your damage? It's too early for you to be this loud." Toby, stood at the top of the stairs rubbing his eyes. He pushed his messy brown hair off his forehead and glared, clearly annoyed at me for waking him up before noon.

My brother was a year younger than me, but stood almost a head taller.

"I don't know," I mumbled, numbly returning my focus back to my dad's face. How do you tell someone that you saw alien ships landing without sounding utterly insane?

"What was that noise?" he demanded, worry creasing his forehead.

I locked eyes with him and waited until my breathing slowed. Swallowing hard, I finally found my voice. "Ships."

"Ships?" Toby scoffed, bumping my shoulder as he passed me on his way to the kitchen.

I knew they wouldn't understand if I told them what I saw. They had to see for themselves. I moved past my dad and jumped over the couch, not giving either of them time to scold me. There was no way it wouldn't be on the news.

I flipped on the television and surfed through the channels, looking for a report as I ignored my parents' constant questions wanting to know what had happened.

It wasn't long before I found a story. The reporter was standing in front of a barricade that blocked people from the massive ship, pointing and describing the landing.

An hour later, the four of us were still sitting on the couch watching the same report that had replayed a dozen times already. We continued to sit, not speaking for hours.

At the time, my mind couldn't formulate the words to put a single coherent thought together. Though now it seemed to be the easiest thing to describe.

Ships had landed in our city. And from the ever-increasing headlines on the ticker at the bottom of the screen, they'd landed all across the world as well.

It was strange, how they stood motionless.

Looking back, it didn't seem so miraculous. Once the ships became silent, nothing, and no one, disembarked from them. It was almost as if they were pretentious art structures that had appeared during the middle of the night, unknown to anyone who had put them there, just something designed to make the populous think.

After a while, that's what many people theorized had happened.

For two years, they sat unmoving under constant supervision. There were shows and programs created around them as the world tried to figure out what they were, why they were here, and who had put them there. The military tested them, but they were as innocuous as a blade of grass. After many failed attempts, they still couldn't get them to open, or even move—though they denied trying.

But I suppose solid metal objects can only hold the attention of the world for so long before they occupied their minds with other things besides shaky cell phone videos and blurry pictures.

After a while, the newspapers started calling it an elaborate hoax. The ones in questionable neighborhoods were graffitied, and they lost all appeal. The ships had simply become part of our scenery.

Even I had turned into one of the skeptics doubting what I thought my own eyes had seen as my feet pounded the pavement two years later.

I took a detour from my normal path and headed around the park, pausing when the gleaming metal of a ship finally forced me to pay attention to it. I had always tried to ignore them. I still don't know what it was about that day that made me take the deviation in my route.

All this time—if you ignored the grass and plants that had grown and were climbing up the tripod landing gear of the legs, which kept the ship suspended—it looked as though it had been there for only minutes. No dust, dirt, or rust marred the mirror like surface of metal.

A chill raced down my spine as I passed. Picking up speed, I headed to the far side of the park to create as much distance between it and me as I could.

I couldn't explain why it made me uneasy at the time. Since the moment it landed, it had never moved or even made a noise, just like every other ship in the world. But being that close gave me the distinct impression of something, or someone inside, watching me—which was ludicrous. It was a solid form without windows.

When I reached the opposite side of the park, a low pulsing rumble hit my ears, and the sound of a distant base froze me in place. It wasn't a high-pitched sound, no whirring or grinding, just the low rumble that was almost too quiet to hear.

My stomach rolled. I could have easily told myself it was just someone playing their music loud and continued on, but instead, I turned to look over my shoulder, pulling my earbuds from my ears.

The ship pushed pressurized air out from beneath it, causing the long blades of grass to sway like ocean waves.

Slowly, the main body of the ship lowered on its legs until it was flush with the ground. It continued blowing out air for hours, the whole time keeping me hostage in my fear.

Fear of the unknown, fear of what lay inside, and fear of how stupid I was to let myself doubt what I'd seen with my own eyes.

The world came running.

Light from the setting sun tinted the ship a rich shade of deep red before leaving us to stare at it in the darkness left by the rapidly fading light.

News crews pushed forward as much as they could, barely restrained by police lines. The din of chatter became a steady drone.

Dark, heavy clouds moved in, swallowing up the last of the

sun's rays. While the crowd had thinned in the last few hours, I'd stayed, unable to drag myself away. I needed to see what, if anything, came off that ship. I needed to know my first instinct was right before I'd let society convince me I hadn't seen one land.

The deep hum of the engine increased as a thin red line lit up around the circumference of the two-story house-sized structure.

My legs shook from the rush of adrenaline coursing through me as I watched a hatch open in the narrow part of the ship. The metal reformed into floating disks, providing a long staircase.

First, legs appeared, then bodies. Normal, *human* looking legs and bodies. No tentacles, no scales… I would have thought an alien race would have a different form, even if their home planet resembled earth in some way. And then their faces were unveiled from the dark shadows of the ship.

An audible gasp from the crowd filled the air, but every inch of the aliens had distinctly human attributes. Even from my vantage point on the far side of the park, groans could be heard, which I assumed were disappointment in the distinctly non-alien appearance of our visitors.

The disembarkment line continued, and no one spoke or made any more noise.

Then, he stepped off the ship. I'm still not sure what it was about him that caught my eye. *Besides the obvious.* He was the same as the others who came before and after him, eerily human. The only thing that set them apart was the fact that their movements held a perfect grace, as though they moved seamlessly through water.

This has to be a hoax, I thought as they disembarked down the ramp. A hush had fallen over the crowd as the men… *aliens,* descended into our midst. High-collared white lab coats hung from their shoulders, opened in the front in a curiously causal manner.

Once the last had set foot on the earth, they stopped in unison, looking over the sea of people that surrounded them.

They stood, on average, a head taller than most of those silently observing with stoic expressions while reporters and bystanders shouted questions at them, though they didn't seem to notice.

The mayor approached. He looked visibly shaken and pale, a sheen of sweat made his skin shine. Part of me expected them to sprout tentacles and eat the closest people to them, another part of me expected them to brandish ray guns and disintegrate the crowd in seconds, what I didn't expect was for them to have a firm grasp of our language.

Mayor Calus held his hand out to one of the aliens who stood in front of the others. Ignoring it, the leader bowed, leveling his face with the portly man, who represented the people of this city, and spoke to him.

I couldn't hear from where I stood so I wove my way through the masses.

People let me pass as they watched on, too busy trying to

take pictures with their cell phones to pay attention to the short girl slipping by.

"…wish to offer peace," the head alien spoke. There wasn't a hint of an accent, which didn't seem possible, not if it was real.

The mayor straightened his back and features at the perfect use of our language, and he muttered a response I couldn't make out.

"I am Thral'el of the Vor'on," the leader spoke.

A younger man stood at Thral'el's side, a few steps behind with his hands clasped at his lower back.

Pathetically, I let him steal my attention. I mean, how was it that the obvious subordinate of the aliens' leader could make me pay more attention to him than the important things happening around me?

Maybe it was my brain's way of coping with the disbelief of everything, trying to hold on to the last fragile strand of what I knew of as reality, I'm still not sure.

I studied his profile. His features were average and very human. He slicked his dark hair back with the same perfection used when he ironed the crisp lines into his clothing, which were tailored to fit his body immaculately. Nothing seemed out of place. The line of his back was board straight, as if he'd never slouched a day in his life. Then, his head swiveled and a strand of hair fell across his forehead as piercing, amber eyes focused on me.

The color was enough to throw me, and I would have thought

it was nothing more than contacts until I saw the vertical slit of his pupil narrow in a way contacts couldn't account for.

I swallowed hard.

I should have run then—I *would* have run then if I'd known what I know now. All the good gained from this could not outweigh what was to come.

Then again, the good was *damn good*. And considering the end, running wouldn't have made a difference anyway.

CHAPTER TWO

The Invitation

A week passed and I felt like I'd entered into an alternate universe. Every country had been in talks with our "guests" almost non-stop. World peace. That's what they claimed they wanted to give us, but even to my naïve ears it sounded too good to be true.

The governments had already gone public with ways to cultivate crops in any climate, almost nullifying starvation immediately as food already began to grow. So maybe all those promises were true. But all other information was being kept under wraps, at least where wars were concerned.

There has been a war somewhere in the world for almost all of written history… so *how* could they possibly prevent war? Though, that too, had been one of their promises.

There was talk of integrating them into our everyday society starting immediately. It was exciting yet somewhat scary. I mean, who wouldn't want the chance to meet an alien?

When I'd first heard the news, I'd been against the idea. Dad's ranting about how everyone rushing to accept them had increased my anxiety. But after a few hours in my room attempting to make progress on my homework, I'd had a chance to form my own opinions, apart from what adults had. Why would they waste their time helping us if all they really wanted was our planet? At least considering that if they had the ability to save us from the major problems plaguing the world, they certainly had the ability to destroy us before we knew what had happened.

The problems on the paper in front of me soon turned into a blur and were replaced with an intense curiosity. The government would begin integrating the Others into our society within the next few weeks.

"Ray," my father called, his voice muffled by the classical music flowing into my ears. I pushed back my headphones so they hung around my neck.

"Raylinn!" he called again.

Shutting my calculus textbook, I scooted my chair away from my desk and walked to the top of the stairs. I leaned over the banister to see my dad frowning as he waited for me next to the open door.

A stern man in a suit stared up at me, his face void of all expression. Mom waited at his side, looking from me to my dad.

Toby leaned against the doorframe, his arms folded over his chest, watching our guest with skepticism. No one spoke, but the look on everyone's face told me I needed to join them. *Now.*

I skipped down the flight of stairs, two at a time, holding onto the banister so I wouldn't trip in my sudden nervousness.

The tension in the room grew suffocating. *Had I done something wrong?* My mind scanned over the last year of everything I'd done, trying to remember if I unwittingly did something illegal, even when I knew I hadn't. *Gotta love good old fashioned paranoia.*

When I reached them, dad placed a hand on my shoulder and then turned to face the suit.

"Is this everyone?"

"Yes," my dad answered through gritted teeth.

The tension between everyone was so thick, I thought I'd choke on it if someone didn't explain what was going on soon.

The man reached into his suit jacket—and of course my imagination went straight to him pulling a gun because he was a hired hit man. But before I could react to my thoughts, he pulled out four large envelopes and handed them out toward my dad, my mom, my brother, and then me. We each took them in turn, not taking our eyes off the man.

"Mr. Marrow, your family has been formally requested to attend the dinner welcoming the Vor'on and thanking them for their ability to guarantee us world peace."

"We never asked for this," my mom spoke up.

The man turned to face her as if only now noticing her. "Invitations were decided upon by lottery. Your presence is *requested*." Even though he wore sunglasses, I could feel the glare behind the lenses, and combined with the emphasis he placed on the last word, I wondered if *requested* was really just code for *mandatory*.

Toby wasted no time opening his, only to give a derisive snort as if it were a joke.

I frowned then looked at my own, reading the script on the envelope. Pulling out the paper inside, I read the details. A ball would be held one week from tomorrow. Families would attend to socialize with the families of the Others as a show of peace and good faith.

An invite to a party? That's what all this fuss was about? I resisted the urge to roll my eyes. *What branch of government hands out invites to a ball?*

"What agency are you with?" I blurted out as I looked up from my invitation. Toby elbowed me in the ribs making me grunt. Ignoring him, I kept my eyes locked on the agent.

"Ray," my dad whispered harshly with an expression that warned me to be quiet.

The suit only turned his covered gaze toward me for a moment that felt much longer than it really was. He didn't speak, just frowned, then looked away.

"Is there anything else we can help you with?" my dad asked curtly.

"If none of you have any questions pertinent to your invitations, then I must be going." He gave us each a cursory glance—not actually allowing us time to speak—nodded his head, then left.

The door shut. I cringed from the near slam and looked at my parents. Mom seemed nervous, but my dad looked furious. I knew he didn't like the idea of aliens among us, but his face was almost red with anger. He snatched the invites out of our hands and ripped them in half.

"What are you doing?" I asked, my jaw dropping open.

"We are not going."

"Can we refuse to go?" my mother asked.

"I wanted to keep that," I said stupidly as I watched him shred the paper in half again and again.

"It doesn't matter, none of us are going." With that, he stormed out of the room, tossing the ripped invitations in the trash.

I got that he didn't like the whole of the situation, but I'd been one of the people picked by chance to go mingle with freaking aliens. It would have at least been nice to have a memento of this weird time of my life. After all, it was highly unlikely they'd stay here forever. Even if they did, this was the beginning of everything. I followed him into the other room.

"It's a once in a lifetime opportunity," I said. "Not everyone got invited."

"Let me ask you this, Ray," my dad started. He'd calmed

down… or at least he'd seemed to have calmed down. His back was to me and his shoulders slumped uncharacteristically as he set his empty water glass down. His hands slid out and gripped the edge of the counter top. "We don't know anything about them. Who knows why they are even here—it's only been a week. How do you know they can be trusted? What if this party we are all invited to turns out to be a trap? Doesn't that seem dangerous?" He finally turned to face me, demanding the answers to his questions. Questions I knew he'd intended to use to sway me to his way of thinking. I just couldn't see it.

"Why would they help us if they just wanted to kill us?" I countered.

His eyes softened. "I don't know. But, it takes time to build trust."

"They are bringing their families too. I don't think anyone would be that heartless to put their kids in danger if they planned to start something." I leaned on the breakfast counter that separated us.

"I don't want to risk either of you in this situation. Everything is still too uncertain. I'd be devastated if I let you go and something did happen." Dad walked around to where I stood and hugged me, placing a kiss on my head. "I love you too much."

I wrapped my arms around him and returned the hug, letting go of the argument. "I love you too, daddy."

I waited until he left the room before walking over to the

trash bin and picking out the ripped up invitation. It was just a souvenir of this time in history. At least that's what I told myself as I slipped the pieces of paper behind a few cereal boxes in the pantry.

After dinner, I was glad I had hidden the scraps earlier. There would have been no retrieving them after the remnants of dinner were piled on top of the garbage. It almost felt intentional with the amount of food my dad had let go to waste. I didn't bring up the topic again, as much as I wanted to, as we sat around the table eating in an awkward silence made worse by the fact that it was anything but quiet every other night. The tension was still palpable.

When I finished, I excused myself and went upstairs to do homework. I stared at the worksheet in front of me, unable to focus. The clock on my nightstand blinked at me, ticking the time away at an agonizingly slow pace.

Lifting my head, the assignment stuck to my cheek for a second before falling to the desk in front of me. I blinked blearily, realizing I'd fallen asleep.

I decided to give up on the homework I hadn't even started for the night and closed the book, pushing back in my chair. I glanced at the clock. It was just after midnight. Five and a half hours had passed since I sat down. I couldn't remember when

I'd fallen asleep.

My muscles ached from sleeping in such a weird and uncomfortable position.

I stood and stretched. For the first time, the house was silent. Crossing the room, I opened my door. All the lights were off. My parents had finally gone to bed.

With light footsteps, I walked across the hall and down the stairs, taking care to avoid the creaking floorboards.

Normally, I wouldn't need to sneak around the house, but I didn't want them to catch me retrieving the very thing my dad made a show of discarding earlier. As I opened the pantry door, it creaked. It seemed so loud to my ears in the quiet house. I paused, waiting to hear my parents stir. When they didn't, I slipped my hand in the narrow opening and felt around for the invitation with my fingers. Grabbing it, I quickly shut the door and rushed up to my room, still trying to be as quiet as possible.

I was almost to my door when my mom stepped out into the hallway.

"Ray, what are you doing up?" she asked, still half asleep.

Shoving the scraps behind my back, I panicked looking for an excuse. "I just had to use the bathroom." The words rushed from my lips, and I scurried into my room before she could reply further. I threw myself onto my bed, placed the paper under my pillow, and shut my lamp off. I waited for her to come in and question me for what felt like forever before realizing she didn't find my behavior half as suspicious as I did.

I clicked the light on again and stood, walking to my desk. I opened the bottom drawer and plucked out a roll of tape. With the pieces of the invitations spread out across the surface of my desk, I sorted through them, looking for the one with my name on it and finding the corresponding segments. I pushed the leftovers in a pile off to the side and set to piecing mine back together.

After placing the final strip of tape, I tried to flatten out the creases with my hands. It was far from perfect, but I could read it well enough.

Whatever agency the suit who'd delivered these was with, they'd certainly put a lot of effort into them. The script looked handwritten. Each letter was expertly placed and written, but the size and strokes weren't identical as they would have been with a font. It really looked as if it had been done by hand.

The ball was next weekend. Masks would be given away at the door when the invitee was to hand over their formal request.

I frowned. *A masked ball? What century was this?*

I wondered if it had something to do with their human like appearance and creating a way for us to meet them without any biases getting in the way. What other reason could they have for holding such a party? It was weird in this day and age. Though the little girl inside me who still longed to be whisked away by prince charming did a little dance at the prospect of it.

A long yawn escaped me. With the excitement of sneaking around the house and piecing together the invitation, I hadn't realized how late it had gotten. Nearly two a.m. I picked up the pieced together paper and walked over to my closet, pulling out an old shoebox I kept on the top shelf in the back. I gently placed my invitation in the box and replaced the lid, returning it to its hiding spot.

I crawled into bed, unable to stop the frown forming on my lips. Even if I'd managed to find a way to get to the ball, there's no way they would have accepted a torn invitation. I hadn't expected to feel so disappointed. It pressed down on my chest with a weight that tugged at the determined side of me begging find a way, regardless.

CHAPTER THREE

The Sighting

The sun warmed my skin and glinted off Miranda's rhinestone sunglasses, nearly blinding me. It was the warmest day we've had so far this year and we didn't want to squander it inside. I pulled my knees to my chest and sat sideways on the seat of the picnic table. Miranda yawned, stretching out on top, her legs dangling over the edge.

"Ugh," Miranda groaned up at the sky. "That test was killer. I think I'd be happy with a D at this point."

I rested my arm on the tabletop just above her head as I twisted my silver bracelet around and around on my wrist, watching the light flicker off the single charm—a shooting star. It had been a gift for my sixteenth birthday from my parents. I always wore it on test days. Perhaps it was a little superstitious, but I considered it my good luck charm.

I laughed. "Don't be ridiculous, you always ace Mr. Rivera's tests. Besides, we'd studied for weeks."

She dropped her head to the side and squinted at me. "I mean it this time, Ray, that test was brutal. A lifetime of studying wouldn't have been enough time to be ready."

I just shook my head and smiled, turning to the grassy field that sprouted up across the park. Small seedlings were pushing their way up, reaching for the sun. She might act like she's the worst student in the world, but she was on track to graduate with a four point average.

A light wind rustled the leaves of the trees that lined the park as birds flitted across the sky, their chirping adding to the gentle harmony of spring, lulling me. My eyelids drooped as the stress of the day melted away.

After a few moments, Miranda pushed up onto her arms. "The party is tomorrow," she said flatly.

I blinked a few times then realized what she meant. The ball to bring aliens and humans together. I'd tried hard not to think about it, but part of me still really wanted to go. Even if the thought of being that close to something that looked so human yet was anything but sent a tendril of fear running along my spine.

"Are you going?" I asked. My stomach twisted with jealousy that she might be able to go.

"Well," she hummed, "my parents don't want to go. They

aren't interested. If I'd gotten an invitation, you can bet nothing would have stopped me."

I twirled my bracelet around my wrist again and again debating on telling her about what had happened to my invitation…

"What's that look?" she asked, narrowing her gaze on me. When I didn't answer she pressed again, "There's something you're not telling me."

"I got an invite." The sun glittered off the delicate silver links as I continued to twist my bracelet.

"You did?" her mouth dropped open. "Why didn't you tell me?"

I shrugged. "I didn't think it mattered. I can't go anyway, Dad ripped them up." She looked at me incredulously, but I continued before she could speak, "I tried to stop him, but you know how stubborn he can be."

Miranda dropped her head back and groaned. "He should be arrested for that," she said teasingly. "What a waste!"

"He wouldn't have let me go, he wouldn't let any of us go." I couldn't help rolling my eyes. He'd always been overprotective. It came from a place of love, so we tried not to fault him for it.

We lapsed into silence for a long moment. I was just about to get up and walk home when I noticed the strange expression on Miranda's face. I turned to look, the murmuring of voices catching my attention.

Three college students walked along the far edge of the

park, two dark-haired men and a woman with a long, fiery braid trailing down her back. I squinted as I watched them casually stroll on, talking to each other. Even from this distance, they were all beautiful. Elegant.

No, not college students—but Others—aliens.

I shifted on the bench, dropping my legs to either side and straddling it. Miranda openly gawked.

They looked… normal, human even. They wandered as casually as anyone else would.

A feminine squeal echoed and I whipped my head to the side to see a girl, only a few years younger than me, standing with her back pressed against the trunk of a tree, reaching out for the book two boys dangled in front of her. Her chin down, she adjusted her large glasses and reached for the book again and again, only to have it yanked out of her reach each time.

I barely had a chance to take in what was happening when the group of three aliens approached them. The two boys from my class spoke sharply to them.

It was then that the Others faced our direction. I sucked in a breath, recognizing one of them, knowing that if he looked up, a pair of warm amber eyes would be peering back.

The girl had crouched down, hugging her knees to her chest. I started to stand, not sure what was about to happen. My palms grew slick as I unlocked the screen on my phone, ready to call the police if needed. I took a step forward and stopped as Miranda placed her hand on my arm. She shook her head. A silent plea for me to keep my distance.

Wind rustled the leaves of the trees, making the light dance on the six of them.

Then, the Others placed themselves between the girl and the two boys. The redhead's arm shot out and snatched the book away. Everyone went still. She took one step forward and the boys paled before falling all over themselves to run away.

I silently let out a long breath. Relief that the situation hadn't become something bigger. Something worse.

She handed the book to the crying girl now wiping her eyes. The one with the amber eyes knelt down beside her and held out a hand. I watched as the crying girl took it, letting him help her to her feet. If she, or the Others, spoke in that moment, they were too far and the words too low for me to hear.

"That's not what I was expecting," Miranda murmured as she contemplated them with her arms crossed over her chest. As if more occurred than I had seen.

"What did you think would happen?" I asked.

I placed my phone in my pocket, guilt tugging on me at the assumptions I'd made in that brief moment. My dad's words, the Others could be dangerous, had come back, burning my neck and face. Even after all my protests that they weren't the villains he saw them as, I had still fallen into that narrow minded way of thinking.

The human girl smiled then picked up her bag, placing her book inside, and left.

Miranda shrugged. "Maybe zap them with a ray gun." I raised an eyebrow at her, but she only smirked, eyes glinting with amusement. "Then I'd have a reason to thank them. Those two are such a pain. They tagged the principal's car last week," she added.

I smiled back.

Her expression changed, slowly, morphing into one I knew all too well. She was up to something.

The Others continued walking and I realized that I wanted to go to that dance. More so than I'd thought. They were a mystery I wanted desperately to unfold and understand—these strange beings who seemed so formal, so cold… and yet, acted in such human ways. I wanted to know more, wanted to know how they thought, how they felt, how they lived.

But I couldn't. Even if by some grace Dad had changed his mind, I no longer had an invitation. That knowledge soured my stomach, turning my mood foul.

"Let's go," I said.

The carpet of grass under my shoes was soft and I enjoyed the feel of it, so much nicer than the squash of mud from overly rainy winters. I tried to let the beautiful day, the soft breeze, ease my disappointment as we left.

But it wasn't enough. I glanced back over my shoulder and found the one with amber eyes meeting my gaze.

He stopped short, his two companions continuing on without him, not noticing he'd been distracted. He stood so still while the world swayed with the wind around him.

I swallowed. Then I turned away, unable to stand the intensity of his eyes bearing down on me.

Miranda and I walked mostly in silence after we'd gone over what we just saw. Whatever hesitation I'd held seemed to dissipate. The Others hadn't noticed us until after the fact, so helping the girl had been something they felt was right and not something to manipulate the feelings of humans around them. The more I thought about it, the more I wanted to learn about them.

It wasn't until we were several blocks away that I noticed my bracelet had fallen off my wrist. I reached out and grabbed my friend's arm.

She faced me, questions swirling in the liquid mahogany of her eyes. "What's wrong?"

"I lost my bracelet," I said, my mouth suddenly dry.

Miranda glanced at her watch. "It's getting late, but we'll retrace our steps."

The pressure on my chest lightened. She never once made fun of my quirks, she just understood they were a part of me.

We searched. And searched. And searched. We traced our steps back the way we'd come and scoured the area around the picnic table we'd sat at. Nothing.

I plopped my butt down on the bench.

"Oh," Miranda squeaked out.

My head shot up, a smile already forming on my face before

it faded. Between her thumb and forefinger was a single silver link. My heart sank.

"Sorry," she said quietly. "We can come back tomorrow and look again, it has to be here somewhere."

"It's okay," I said, taking the broken link and shoving it into the pocket of my jeans. I appreciated the fact that she was willing to come back on a fruitless mission just to ease my heart.

The sun had started to set while we searched. We'd been out later than planned, so I pushed up from the bench and joined her as we rushed to catch the seven fifteen bus.

CHAPTER FOUR

The Decision

The night of the party I sat on the couch, arms crossed over my chest as we watched some movie. I couldn't tell anyone what it was about if they asked as my tumbling thoughts remained on the night I'd be missing out on. If my family noticed my sour mood, no one said anything.

"I'm heading to bed. I think I'm coming down with something," I muttered as I stood. Movie night just wasn't doing it for me this week. The truth was, I was too distracted and too disappointed about not being able to go to the ball.

Freaking aliens! I resisted the urge to pout on the way up to my room.

Letting myself think how I'd hoped to see a specific set of amber eyes, wasn't going to happen. Amber eyes that had been on my mind far more often in the past few weeks then I'd cared to admit. But giving in to those thoughts would only sour my mood even more.

I slipped into a tank top and a pair of thin shorts then curled under the blankets, sighing as I relaxed into the mattress.

The cheerful tune of my ring tone went off. For most of its song, I debated letting it go to voicemail. I wasn't in the mood to talk. Reluctantly I glanced at the caller ID. Miranda. I grumbled. If anyone could cheer me up about this, it was her. Not to mention if I didn't pick up, she'd keep calling until I did.

"Hello?" I muttered into my cell.

"You weren't seriously sleeping, were you?" She knew me too well. I could never hide anything from her. Everything I felt was in the tone of my voice and she was one of the few who could always hear everything.

"I was thinking about it," I admitted. It was only five and even though the sun was still up, I'd shut my curtains and turned off the lights, making it seem like it was the middle of the night.

"Get up and take a shower, I'm coming over. We are going to that party!"

"What?" I sat up straight. I knew that look on her face the day before meant she was up to no good.

"And, put on a bra, Shane is coming with," she said, then hung up the phone not waiting for a response.

I had no idea how she planned to get us into that party. I would find out soon enough I supposed.

Sure enough, twenty minutes later, there was a knock at the front door. I rushed to peek out into the hallway and saw Miranda talking with my dad. I could hear the hesitation in his voice, but with a few bright smiles and a promise not to stay long, she was through the door and on her way up. I quickly backed up as she rushed through the door. She scanned me from head to toe with a frown.

"You haven't dressed yet?" Miranda scolded. "The party starts in an hour. We don't have much time to get you ready." She looked me up and down, frowning as if I'd just been given to her as an assignment.

"My dad will never let me out of the house if he thinks I'm going to the ball." I reminded her. "Besides, I told them I wasn't feeling well."

"Are you sick?" she asked, knowing full well that I wasn't.

I pursed my lips. "No, I was just disappointed."

"Well, that's why I'm here, to fix that." A wicked smile spread across her lips. "Now, how do we get you out of here?"

My gaze traveled from the door to the tree just outside my window. It had been years since I'd climbed down that tree.

I'd never disobeyed my parents in such a big way before. But this was a once in a lifetime opportunity that would never come again, and that was not something I wanted to give up on so easily. *Besides, what harm could it do?*

"I could climb down," I said, not entirely sure I still possessed the skill to do so without falling and breaking every bone in my body. But I pushed that doubt down, refusing to entertain the idea.

"Perfect!" Miranda grinned mischievously, then made a

beeline for my closet.

We'd been friends for years, ever since elementary school when I was still too painfully shy to try making friends. When the teacher told us to pair up for an assignment, I sat there and waited to be put with whoever was left. But Miranda reached out to me and asked me to be her partner. We clicked immediately, becoming inseparable, and ever since then, she'd always had a way of bringing me out of my shell without pushing me too far beyond my limits.

"So, how exactly are we getting into this party when we don't have any invitations?"

"You just leave that up to me," she said, giving me a wink and turning to rummage through my clothes.

"I'm not sure I like the sound of that," I said, crossing my arms and looking at her with one raised brow.

"Ugh, you don't have anything to wear!" Miranda complained. Her head dropped back as she groaned up at the ceiling. She turned and looked at me with an expression that questioned my taste in clothes.

I shrugged and walked up next to her and examined my closet, trying to see what she did. "What are you looking for exactly?"

"Something for a formal occasion."

I snorted. "Right… and when have I ever gone to anything formal?"

"What about prom?"

"It's not for months; the stores have only just put out their dresses. Besides, I'm not even sure I want to go. You know I don't have a date, and I'm not going to be the third wheel with you and Shane."

"You never know… but fine. I think I have a dress that will fit you." Miranda dropped to the floor and began shifting through my piles of shoes until she stopped on a pair of red heels I bought on a whim during the summer but still hadn't had a chance to wear. Once she found those, she moved on to rummage through my jewelry box and picked something out, then grabbed my makeup bag on the vanity and shoved everything in a small gym bag she'd found at the bottom of my closet. I didn't even know I had one.

Miranda shoved the bag in my hand and headed toward the door. "Shane and I will drive around the corner and meet you there. Hurry, we don't have much time to get ready before it starts," she said before walking out.

I walked quietly toward the door and peeked downstairs. She was already at the door talking with my dad, telling him I was about to fall asleep. Then she was gone. My dad closed the door behind her, walked back into the living room, and resumed the movie. I didn't move until I heard the noise from the movie.

Quietly, I shut the door and debated on locking it. If I locked it and my parents tried to open it, they might pound on it only to find out I wasn't home, but leaving it unlocked… there was a chance they'd either stick their heads in or come kiss me on my forehead and then discover I was gone.

A frown pulled at the corners of my mouth. Unlocked was

still my best chance. I made my way over to the bed and shoved some pillows under the blankets. I felt like a kid.

What am I doing? I thought. Sneaking around wasn't exactly the mature thing to do. *Is going to this ball really that important to me?* A pair of amber eyes flashed in my mind.

I wanted to go *for me*, to do what I wanted and not worry about what someone else wanted for me, and honestly, I just wanted to see those eyes again. I wanted to ask him the endless questions circling my mind that had been multiplying since they landed, doubling since the day before at the park, wanted to know these Others, and have the curiosity that made sleeping near impossible, satiated.

With one last tug on the blankets, I took a step back and examined my work. If I didn't know better, I'd swear that there was someone sleeping in my bed.

I put my bag over my shoulder, slipped a pair of shoes on, then made my way to the window. Balancing on the short, steep slope of the ledge outside my window, I took one last look over my shoulder. I hesitated, second-guessing myself for a brief moment. I shook off the feeling and turned toward the branch that reached toward the house. I grabbed on to the one above and walked myself to the trunk.

Once safely on the ground, I spared a glance up, trying to memorize the best climbing path back. After all, it would be dark when I returned. The sun was already setting.

The second my foot hit the soil, I stopped doubting my decision and fully embraced going after what I wanted. It was almost as if the desire to attend the ball and spend one night among the aliens spurred me on.

I took off running through my back yard, the neighbors, and out into the street behind my house. I looked both ways, spotting Miranda and Shane to my left. I raced toward the car as they drove to meet me in the middle. Only once we were around the corner did I let myself breathe a sigh of relief.

Shane drove like a crazy person until we reached Miranda's house. I hated when he drove, but I was just happy that I didn't usually get car sick, and she only lived a few blocks away. We reached her house in record time.

The two of us got out of the car. Miranda leaned over and stuck her head through the open window. "Meet us back here in an hour —" she paused and looked at me then back to Shane. "And a half."

Clearly, I had some cleaning up to do.

"So, how are we going to get into the ball? You know my dad ripped up my invitation," I asked again as we approached her house.

She grabbed my forearm and stopped me. "My parents aren't going either... and neither is Shane's mom. So, he and I will be Mr. and Mrs. Larson, and you will be Ms. Morin."

My smile dropped. "I'm going to be his *mother*?"

"Only in name," she said, continuing to walk. I hurried to catch up with her. "No one will know but us."

I had to admit it wasn't a terrible plan. It was almost too coincidental, really. All our parents not wanting to go had ended up making this easy for us.

My excitement to attend renewed as we made our way to Miranda's room with her talking nonstop about how great the night would be.

The moment she stepped through her door, she was a tornado of activity. I had no idea where to start so I just sat on the foot of her bed and waited. She threw open her closet and started pushing clothes aside, pulling dresses from the back and tossing them to me. Once she was finished, we looked them over.

Most were way too short for my tastes, or too low cut. I couldn't pull off half of these even if I'd wanted to.

"Uhhg!" she groaned, resting her fists on her hips as she frowned down between the mounds of fabric spread out across the bed and me. I knew what she was thinking. The ones that would fit me wouldn't be appropriate for a ball, and the ones that were... well the fit wouldn't work with me. I had considerably less to work with than Miranda did.

I raised an eyebrow and looked at her from the corner of my eyes. "It's okay," I started.

"Oh!" The sudden cry startled me as she gripped my shoulders and brought her face close to mine. Her eyes went wide with excitement. "Wait here. I have *just* the dress for you!" she said as she ran from the room.

When she returned, she was carrying a garment bag in both arms. Miranda closed the door behind her with her foot.

"Now, this is my mom's, she's petite like you, but..." She glanced over her shoulder before continuing. "I swear it was made for you."

"Won't your mom notice it's missing?" I asked.

"No, besides, we'll have it back before she could possibly have any reason to look for it." Miranda unzipped the bag, pulling out a silky, deep ocean blue, floor length dress and held it out to me. Crystal beading made a stunning lace design that wrapped around the waist, crossed between the center of the bodice, and over the single shoulder strap on the left.

"It's beautiful," I breathed. It looked so expensive, I was almost afraid to touch it.

"Hurry and get ready," she said, shoving the garment in my arms and turning toward the bathroom with her own dress in hand.

We finished getting ready just as Shane pulled up to the house and honked. I put the top back on my lip-gloss and stepped back to take a quick glance at my reflection in the mirror. The dress hugged my curves in a way my normal clothes never did. I ran my hands through my hair one last time to smooth out a few stray pieces and followed my friend from the room.

The sun continued to set as we slid into the car.

"Wow, babe, you look… hot," Shane said as he reached for Miranda.

"You clean up pretty good yourself," she murmured, leaning into him.

"You can grab each other's butts later; we have a party to get to." I interrupted them, knowing that if I didn't say anything I'd end up with a front row seat to a make out session, and I did not need to see that.

They pulled apart and she gave me a sheepish look over her shoulder before turning back to watch him.

I don't know if it was nerves at sneaking around, or the excitement at seeing aliens. Maybe it was a mixture of everything, but the drive to the Alabaster House went fast. It was the city's large, historical building, popular for upscale weddings and parties that the upper class held. I wasn't born to a silver spoon family, so I never had the connections to hang out at the country club before.

My phone buzzed. I frowned, pulling it from my pocket. The only one who ever texted me was Miranda. I looked at my screen. *Toby.*

Crap! He never messaged me... *what could he want?* I wondered.

I opened his message and my stomach seemed to fill with lead.

Chapter Five

The Beginning

I know what you did. Toby's cryptic message read.

I waited a long moment before replying, trying to decide if I should threaten him, or play innocent. I bit my lip and typed out my response.

Leave me alone. I'm sleeping.

Where did you go?

What are you talking about?

My heart pounded. He was just messing with me. He had to be. After all, he'd known how much I wanted to go. Toby gave me a hard time about it all week saying I just wanted to see a freak show.

My room is right next to yours, loser. I saw you sneak out.

"Whoa, are you all right, Ray? You look super pale."

I looked up to see Miranda staring at me with her dark chocolate eyes clouded with concern. She was like a classic movie star with her hair pinned to the side in perfect, smooth waves. The red starlet dress and white gloves against her dark brown skin made her stand out. Everyone would be looking at her tonight.

I finally managed to find my tongue. "Yeah, it's nothing. I'm just excited," I lied.

She looked at me for another long moment before turning back around. It was too late for me. I might have been caught, but I wasn't about to ruin my friend's night too. If I was going to get in trouble for going to the ball, I might as well go and enjoy it. The punishment would be the same either way.

Do Mom and Dad know?

I texted Toby again, nervous he'd already spilled about me leaving. For the most part, we got along, but we still had our spiteful fights. And this was something that could easily turn into one of *those* moments if he was in the wrong mood.

Minutes ticked by with no response. I could feel my hands begin to shake from the adrenaline that was pumping through my veins. Instantly, I began to regret my decision to sneak out. I never did anything like that, not for years, and never anything this big. What had I been thinking? A cool sweat broke out over my forehead as I waited for his response.

Damn it, Toby! Did you tell them?

Lol. Chill sis.

Are you going to tell them?

That depends on you.

I glared at the phone in my hands as I fought to stay calm. He really knew how to push my buttons. After several deep breaths, my heart had slowed down enough so I could breathe again. I gave in to his game and replied with the five words that I knew he wanted from me.

Tell me what you want.

Now you're talking. My chores for a month.

No way!

Have fun with mom and dad later. :)

He could have been bluffing, but at that moment, I didn't want to take that chance. I was too close to freedom. It figured, the one time I did anything slightly rebellious my pain-in-the-butt brother would catch me and blackmail me.

You owe me for all those times I covered for you.

*Not my fault you weren't smart enough to
get something out of it.*

I gritted my teeth and texted him back, determined to never let him get away with his antics again.

Fine. I'll do your chores for a month.

He sent me a few more texts composed of stupid victory dance images and smug faces. He was getting too much pleasure out of watching me squirm. With that settled, I ignored him and silenced my phone and sat back, letting my shoulders sag in relief. I was in the clear. At least, so long as Toby kept his end of the bargain. I leaned back against the leather seat and put my cell phone back in my purse just as we were approaching the country club.

Putting thoughts of my brother behind me, I turned to look out my window. Elaborate gardens edged the sides of the building and a half moon-shaped garden out front, and created a horseshoe driveway. We pulled up to the front and got out. Shane handed the keys to one of the valets.

The steps leading up to the entrance were made of marble, giving the finishing touch of elegance to the outer façade.

There was an obvious effort to make the feel of the evening reminiscent of space in honor of our guests, *or in our amusement of them.* Or maybe it was just a misguided attempt to make them feel at home. Regardless, it was beautiful.

If I thought I looked good before leaving, this place made me feel self-conscious. I suddenly felt like a vagabond trying to sneak in as a sea of beautiful people walked by. I thought for sure they would stop us and tell us to go home, but they accepted our invitations without incident and let us pass, handing us each a mask to wear. It itched slightly around the edges when I slipped it on.

Inside was even more elaborate than the outside. The hallway leading to the dining room was dimly lit. Cream-colored material covered the walls, tied to the pillars. At the end of the hall, we entered a large, open room with an expansive ceiling. Round tables were arranged through the room and a platform that held a podium was on the far side. The wall to the right was an open doorway leading to a grand ballroom.

The dinner was uneventful as everyone sat around in identical black masks. Some people, like the mayor and a few other well-known faces, I recognized, but other than that, everyone was dressed in a similar fashion. I looked around when I realized all men wore nearly the exact same thing. About half were gloved, but all wore dark high collar suits, resembling a Mao tunic style jacket.

Turning to Shane, I realized he had one on as well—a detail I'd missed at first. I supposed it made sense for the suits to be similar under the premise of the evening. But it almost seemed as if the men were trying to cover most of themselves.

I wonder what they are trying to hide, I thought.

Throughout dinner, I could hardly take more than a few bites as I half listened to the speeches given by city officials and the only alien I recognized.

Thral'el, the head alien who'd first spoken to mayor Calus. Of course, it was a lot easier to recognize him when he stated who he was.

Though once he stepped back into the crowd, I lost track of him. I don't know how they did it, but even with their taller than average height, they managed to blend in perfectly.

The speeches varied on topic, but remained centered on the need to come together and work as equals. How we needed to put aside fears and work together for peace.

Then the mayor went on to reiterate what the news had been saying all week. The Others have given us ways to make all soil viable and able to grow almost any crop needed.

It was sometime near the middle of all of this that I felt the hairs on the back of my neck stand on end. I couldn't focus on what he was saying. I only caught a few words here or there. Borders. No war. No weapons. *Safe*.

All throughout, I had the feeling of being observed. It was a steady presence, increasing with each passing second.

Finally, the speeches ended and quiet, but excited, murmuring filled the room. I would have taken part, what had been talked about was thrilling, but I just couldn't shake the ever increasing feeling of being watched.

As people finished their dinner, they stood and began mingling throughout the room. I swallowed hard, trying to push this sudden unnerved feeling down and reached for my glass of water. I wasn't usually this paranoid.

My eyes darted around the room, trying to pinpoint the source. I stopped as my gaze landed on the face of a man three tables away. My heart pounded against my ribs in an uneven rhythm. I wiped the palm of my hand on the cloth napkin on my lap.

He sat among a table mixed with humans and Others, but rather than eating or talking as everyone else, he stared directly at me. I could feel the heat from his gaze. It was uncomfortable under his scrutiny, and I wished he would look somewhere else.

I wasn't paying attention and the tips of my fingers brushed against my glass with too much force, knocking it over. The chime of the crystal on my neighbor's plate sounded defining, even through the din of chatter.

I cringed as the water splashed and could have sworn every set of eyes in the room turned toward me.

CHAPTER SIX

The Dance

"I'm so sorry," I murmured to the woman next to me as I dabbed at the spill with my napkin. My face burned and I could still feel the man's stare. She told me it was okay while helping me wipe up the mess.

"Are you okay?" Miranda asked looking concerned.

I was still beyond embarrassed and nodded as I fought to hide the blush that now blazed across my face.

Pushing my chair back, I stood. "I just need some air."

I wove my way through groups of people who had finished dining and were now mingling timidly with other guests as if they wanted to pretend this was the same as every other day and we were not surrounded by aliens.

My shoes clacked on the floor, echoing throughout the large, empty space of the ballroom. In the back of my mind, I knew spilling my water wasn't a big deal, but with those eyes staring so intently from across the room, I felt as though the attention of the entire world was upon me.

From where I stood, I could see the open doors that lined the wall on the far side, leading out to the back gardens. Lights adorned the trees and fountains lining the pathway. Warm string lights were scattered around the room and reflected off the shining, black floor, making it feel as if we were in a cruise liner in space. Much like the rest of the building, there were swaths of thin cream and black fabric tied to columns, draping from ceiling to floor. Sets of French doors ran along the outside wall, spaced evenly between each pillar.

Once outside, I took a deep breath and willed my pounding heart to slow.

"Ray?" Miranda's voice called softly from behind me.

I looked over my shoulder as she stepped out onto the veranda.

"Are you okay? You ran out of there really fast."

"Yeah," I said, pretending to examine my nails. "I was just embarrassed."

She looped her arm through mine, bumping shoulders with me. "Hardly anyone noticed. Come on, let's go back inside, people are starting to move to the ballroom!" she practically sang the last part.

I smiled, letting her infectious energy influence me. I had wanted to come to this dinner since we got our invitations.

It was silly for me to hide because I spilled a little water. I knew it wasn't my lack of grace that had me on edge, but the intense stare that had been locked on me. Now that I was away from the weight of it, I questioned if it was all in my mind. At the time, I'd assumed he was an alien, but maybe I was wrong. I hadn't looked at him long, and for all I knew, he was someone who knew me through my father instead of the alien who might have been trying to see if he recognized me from the day they finally left their ships… or from the day before at the park.

What other reason was there for staring at someone like that?

Miranda dragged me into the thick of the crowd that had formed in the few minutes I'd been outside. A string quartet was warming up in the corner of the room as the lights dimmed.

We made our way along the wall to where Shane waited.

"My lady," he said, bowing to Miranda as we approached. "May I have this dance?"

She let go of my arm and took his hand. Looking back, she smiled. "Dance, have fun. I'll be back after this song."

I watched her walk into the center of the room as the music started. The swirling dresses moving to the orchestra was like a scene straight out of a fairy tale.

"Raylinn?" a vaguely familiar voice said my name hesitantly.

I turned to look at a young man. The crooked smile looked familiar, but I couldn't place where I knew him from.

"It's me," he said, lifting his mask to show his face as if that would be enough for me. "Josh, we're in calculus together."

He smiled while the information slowly clicked into place.

"Oh, hey Josh." Relief washed over his features when I finally realized who he was. Though, I wasn't sure what to say. We sat next to each other in math class, but other than that, we didn't have much interaction.

"I didn't think I'd see anyone I knew here." He looked out at the dancers then back at me with a look I couldn't decipher.

"Yeah, me either." I let out a nervous laugh and let our conversation lapse into a slightly awkward silence.

"Do you want to dance?" Josh asked after a moment.

I ignored the question, not sure if I felt comfortable enough with him. *Would he take it as a sign that I liked him?* He was a nice guy, but he was quiet and not really my type. The last thing I wanted to do was lead him on. I thought that maybe excusing myself would be the best option.

The song ended as I opened my mouth to answer. Just then, Miranda and Shane walked into view with broad smiles. Her grin grew when she saw Josh standing next to me.

"So?" Josh asked again as another song started up. "Did you want to dance?"

"She'd love to!" Miranda volunteered an answer for me.

At that point, I didn't know how to refuse without making the situation worse, so I took his arm and let him lead me out onto the dance floor.

Within minutes, I regretted it. Josh was a sweet guy, but a terrible dancer. My feet ached, and I wasn't sure if he'd broken a toe or two from stepping on my feet so many times. Though, once I angled my body further away from him to avoid any more accidental missteps, I started to get into the music, even laughing along with him once the feeling returned to my toes.

We narrowly avoided other couples as we made up our own steps to the music, not caring if we looked utterly ridiculous, until we bumped into another couple.

The woman frowned at us in disapproval. Her face pinched from her narrowed eyes to her pursed lips. And the man—no, *alien*—that accompanied her just tilted his head.

Still high from the fun we'd been having, I stuck out my tongue playfully and winked. I wouldn't let a simple misstep ruin the night.

Josh laughed and led me away. We danced to a few more songs. All the while, I had felt the weight of eyes on me. I chalked it up to the presence of the aliens and the almost tangible aura that surrounded the Others.

After a few spins around the room, I had come to recognize them by the buzz of energy they put off. It made the air around them come alive.

I pulled away from Josh, breathless.

"I need water," I said, fanning myself with my hand. I stepped in between several couples and wove my way through the masses until I reached the edge of the room, heading toward a table in the back.

So many people stood around the table that reaching one of the drinks would take more effort than I'd felt like giving. It was too hot to fight my way through such a densely packed crowd.

Turning on my heel to change directions, I nearly ran into

someone.

"Excuse me," I muttered, not looking up as I continued to walk.

A hand brushed along my arm, making me come to an abrupt stop. My feet cemented to the floor. Familiarity was in the caress, but I had no idea who would know me well enough to touch me yet keep walking. I turned to look, but whoever it was had already been lost to the throng.

The earlier feeling of being watched returned. I wondered if it was the same man. Scanning the room, I couldn't find anyone even paying attention to me.

I shook it off and made my way outside. A few deep breaths later and the feeling once again vanished.

The cool breeze of the night air felt good on my overheated skin as I walked down the steps and into the gardens. The smooth path wound around, weaving in and out from between trees, tall flowering bushes, and several fountains. It was as if I'd stepped into a completely different world than I'd grown up in. One that held mystery and magic. I'd been to a flower garden when I was younger, but it paled in comparison to this.

I followed the sound of running water to a small stream rolling over a perfect arrangement of rocks. The sun had set sometime during the dinner and speeches, and the stars had come out twinkling above.

I pushed my mask off my face, letting it slide from between my fingers and drop to the ground. Tilting my head back, I looked up at the stars. They seemed brighter on this hill above the city where there was distance from the light pollution. The thick band of the Milky Way was like a streak of magic dust trailing out from an unknown spell.

"What are you looking at?" a man asked.

The question surprised me and my heel caught on the uneven ground, knocking me off balance. A gloved hand reached out, wrapping around my waist and keeping me from falling. I straightened and pulled myself free from his arm that had pressed me against his body.

He was so close; my eyes were level with the spot where the notch of his clavicle sat in the center of his neck. I lifted my eyes and saw a warm smile below his black mask obstructing my view of his eyes. I didn't have to see them to know they were a piercing amber.

He backed up once he was no longer holding on to me. "Do you have trouble adjusting to your planet's gravity?" he asked.

I blinked a few times before I realized what he meant.

"No, you just startled me." Nervously, I smoothed out the blue fabric of my dress. When I looked back at him, his head was tilted toward the sky. I cleared my throat. "Are you really an alien?"

He dropped his chin and faced me, his features covered by shadow. He reached up and removed his mask, then let it fall to the ground next to mine.

My heart hammered in my chest while I waited for him to say something.

Had I made a mistake? There was a moment of panic where

I doubted my certainty of his Otherness.

"We do not think of ourselves as such, but from your point of view, yes." As he spoke, he stepped closer to me until I was forced to look up just to meet his gaze. He was close enough to touch, close enough to wrap my arms around, and if I stood on my toes...

I shook my head. Why was I thinking about being intimate with a stranger, one who wasn't even human? He reached up and pushed a strand of hair behind my ear. His fingertips lingered on my skin, caressing the outer edge of my ear and down my jaw, before his palm cupped my cheek.

"I saw you —" I paused to swallow the lump that formed in my throat. "I saw you watching me earlier."

"You were there yesterday." It wasn't a question. His voice was soft and mesmerizing. With each word, the space between us seemed to dissolve.

I nodded.

He reached into a pocket and a soft, familiar chime drew my attention to the closed fist he held between us. His long fingers unfurled to reveal a delicate silver chain with a single star charm pooled in his palm. The broken link now fixed. I reached for it, my fingers hovering just above the bracelet.

"You... you found it." My gaze shot to his. I had thought it had been lost forever, maybe picked up before I'd noticed it was gone.

"I found it after you left." When I didn't take it he unclasped it and wrapped it around my outstretched wrist, the pads of his fingers brushing my skin. The familiar weight of the bracelet was comforting.

I didn't ask how he knew it was mine. Perhaps he had seen me long before I realized he had.

"Thank you." My voice was barely above a whisper. He leaned in closer… or maybe I'd been the one to close that distance. "What are you doing?" I asked.

There was something about him that, even as he lowered his face and rested his forehead against mine, made the world tilt around me. I closed my eyes and inhaled his warm scent. I felt a pull in my core, as if someone had woven a thread through me and was drawing me to him. My chest pressed against his as his mouth brushed against my cheek. My lips parted, releasing a small gasp. The warmth of his breath sent chills over my body.

"I don't even know who you are," I managed to say weakly, hardly recognizing my own voice as the words came out airy.

"Raylinn?" Josh's voice jolted me back to reality.

I blinked and took a step back, trying to shake off the lingering effects of his touch. Golden eyes with a vertical pupil stared at me, free from the shadows of the mask.

There were so many questions I had for the man in front of me. I wasn't ready to give up on this stolen moment. Grabbing his hand, I moved us into the shadows, just off the side between various plants and trees. I chanced a look away from his curious, otherworldly gaze, to see Josh walking down the path toward the spot we'd been standing in moments ago.

The alien pulled me farther into the shadows, away from the

main path. Perhaps this stranger felt the same and wasn't ready to relinquish our time together. He leaned against a tree, and I stumbled over a root and into him.

I smiled, almost giving our position away by speaking. The tips of his fingers covered my mouth as he returned the expression.

I peeked around him. Josh had picked up our masks and was looking around. Part of me felt terrible for ditching him, but then we had just ran into each other here. We hadn't come as dates.

I held my breath as he walked closer to our alcove. Josh paused at the tree line and took one step in, then paused.

So many thoughts raced through my mind, competing to be the most important of them. Would he find us? What did it matter if he did? What would it mean? What would happen? What would everyone think, despite the reasoning for tonight's events?

Josh took one more step forward, squinting into the dark. His shoulders slumped in disappointment. I bit my lip at seeing his frown. But before I could think more on it, he turned on his heel and walked back toward the music.

Once Josh was gone, and I was alone with the alien again, I let myself breathe as I rested my forehead against his chest.

I didn't know him. But in that moment, the fact that he was a stranger to me, and not even human… well it didn't seem to matter. I lifted myself up on my toes, bringing my lips closer to his. His breath brushed softly against my skin, making my body come alive. It was intoxicating being this close.

"Raylinn?" Miranda's voice called, echoing across the courtyard.

I tried to ignore the voice that threatened to pull me from the incredible moment, but once it entered my consciousness, it drew me out despite my attempts at hiding. I let out a groan, both of pleasure and pain, as I pulled away.

Seeing my distraction, he dropped his hands from my waist, taking the warmth with his embrace.

"That was unusual," he said, his voice thick with passion.

Though the words were odd, the way in which he spoke made it clear it wasn't meant in a negative light. In fact, his tone implied the opposite. I'd obviously never met an alien before, and it surprised me that I allowed myself to be drawn into someone so completely.

We knew nothing about each other. But I wanted to believe we were the same. Maybe his home planet was more like a superhero's world from one of those old comics.

Or maybe the concept of alien was just a cover for the world's scientists, a way to give the world the technology it so desperately needed while also inserting a level of fear into society in order to maintain stricter control over the population.

My imagination went wild trying to justify what I'd felt in a way my brain could handle. Though in the end, who he was, and the reasons behind it, didn't matter. If I'd been told everything had happened because of magic, I would have gladly accepted the explanation.

"Ray? Where are you? We need to go!"

I looked toward my friends as they ventured closer, then back at the alien who had stolen my attention. I'd been so caught up in the rapture of the moment I had lost my head. And even knowing that, I still didn't want to relinquish the feeling that had pulled me into its clutches and held me captive.

Hesitation rooted me to the spot. I knew I had to go, but…

"Find me," I said, giving his hand a squeeze before letting it fall from my fingers and turning to run toward my friends.

CHAPTER SEVEN

The Kiss

I left him standing in the shadows. I couldn't be sure, but I think he wanted to explore the moment we shared as much as I did, without the interference of outside opinion to taint it.

Miranda and Shane caught up to me by the fountain, looking at me with wide eyes.

"Hey, Ray, what happened to your mask?" Shane asked.

"My mask?" My hand shot to my face. I had forgotten all about it. "Oh, it was bothering me so I took it off."

"Come on, we need to get home before my parents get back," Miranda said, taking my hand and leading me away. Shane followed behind.

I was in disbelief. Had I actually told him to find me? Would he be able to? There were so many questions I wanted to ask him, so many things I wanted to know… and after running off like I had, it didn't seem possible I'd ever see him again. It was almost impossible for us to find each other in this city by chance again. We knew nothing about each other. At that realization, my heart sank and my smile started to slip from my face.

Unzipping the bag I'd left in the car, I pulled out a tee and a pair of jeans. I managed to change stealthily into my street clothes by ducking low behind the driver's seat. Once out of the dress, I felt more like myself again. Though I loved the dress, it didn't feel like *me*.

I folded the beautiful blue gown up as gently as I could and passed it to Miranda. She took it without much thought as she gushed about the food and the dancing on the way home. I did my best to join in, but my memory of the night seemed only to be filled with bright amber eyes, soft touches, and an almost kiss.

The car pulled to a stop, and I glanced up to find Miranda looking at me strangely because I'd grown quiet. I faked a yawn and Miranda seemed pacified. I quickly got out of the car, slinging my bag over my shoulder.

"I'll call you in the morning!" Miranda said with her head out the window as Shane pulled away.

I waited until they were around the corner before cutting through the neighbor's yard. Sticking to the shadows at the edge of my lawn I hurried to the tree outside my room. Climbing down was one thing, but having to go back up was another matter. I gripped on to some lower branches and pulled myself up, hoping

I hadn't lost the skill to avoid falling and breaking my neck.

It was slow, and I ended up with far more scratches and bruises than I'd had in a long time, but I eventually made it safely to the window.

The low thumping of music started in Toby's room as I gripped the windowsill and started to pull myself in. Two strong hands gripped my wrists and pulled and it was all I could do not to cry out as I was hauled inside.

"Could you be any louder?" Toby asked in a harsh whisper. He helped steady me as I dragged my legs into my room.

"What are you doing in here?" I snapped, annoyed he was in my room. I plopped down on my knees as I started pulling leaves from my hair.

"Making sure you didn't die getting back inside." Toby sat on the foot of my bed. "We both know how weak your arms are."

"Gee, thanks." I could have made it even if he beat me at arm wrestling within seconds every time.

"So, what have you been up to?" he asked nonchalantly leaning against the wall.

I stopped picking debris out of my hair and glanced at him. His expression smug, as if he knew something I didn't. "I went to the ball," I said curtly.

A look of disgust crossed his face. "Dressed like that?"

"I'm not that fashion challenged," I rolled my eyes and went back to pulling stray twigs from my tangled nest. "I borrowed a dress from Miranda."

"Did you meet anyone?" he asked in a strained voice. If I didn't know better, I'd say he was almost worried about me.

"Mmm," I shrugged. "I saw someone from class." While I didn't lie, I hadn't exactly told the truth. Part of me just didn't want to share the short stolen moment, and I wasn't sure if it counted as meeting someone if we never introduced ourselves.

We sat in silence for a while before he stood and stretched.

"Night, punk," he said, messing my hair as he passed me. The door clicked closed softly behind him.

The clock next to my bed read one o'clock in the morning already. I hadn't realized we'd been out so late, and I hoped Miranda had made it home before her parents did. The thought to text her and ask crossed my mind, but if she'd been caught it would only make things worse for her, and condemn me as well. I'd talk to her in the morning.

I changed into the shorts and tank top I'd worn earlier and placed my bracelet in my jewelry box. I frowned at my bed. I wasn't tired. My energy had spiked due to the night's excitement.

Light from the full moon streamed into my room, filtered by the leaves of my tree, creating wild shapes that danced across the floor.

Pushing my window open, I sat on the edge and stared up at the stars. I wondered which was the one that warmed the Other's world. I wondered what their planet looked like. Was it like ours, or did it look like something out of a science fiction movie?

A movement below caught my eye, and I clamped a hand

over my mouth. I squinted into the dark and could only make out the outline of a man's figure.

It couldn't be... I thought.

"Psst," I hissed down. He stepped into the light and my breath caught. He had found me, just as I'd told him too. I'd never thought he'd find me so soon, or even try.

"I found —" he started, but I immediately shushed him. He frowned.

"Can you climb?" I asked, and when he didn't answer, I pointed to the tree.

Without another word, he made his way up between branches in record time. The next thing I knew, I was staring into sparkling eyes. They were otherworldly with yellow specks throughout the iris, exactly how I'd imagine a dragon's eyes to look.

I took a step back and motioned for him to come in. He did so with more grace than I thought possible.

"We should be quiet," I whispered.

He nodded.

My heart pounded. There was a guy in my room in the middle of the night. An *alien* no less, and one I felt an undeniable pull toward.

I knew I was treading dangerous waters, but I wouldn't have been able to stop myself even if I'd wanted to.

He stood next to the window and watched me, waiting for me to make a move.

I walked up to him and took his hand, then looked to my bed.

No, I knew that would have been taking a huge risk considering what being near him did to me. Standing was probably the safest thing. I stopped only a few inches in front of him and had to tilt my head back to look into his eyes. As much as I wanted to continue the moment we shared earlier, I had so many questions.

"What's your name?"

"Jace'el," he stated simply.

When he didn't ask my name in return I offered it up. "I'm Raylinn, but most people call me Ray."

"How would anyone know what house you belong to?" I frowned not understanding. After a long moment he clarified. "What is your house name?"

"House name?" I tilted my head to the side. "My family name is Marrow, if that's what you mean. Raylinn is my first name, and Ray is a nick name."

His eyes narrowed as he took in the information. I could see the confusion in his expression.

"I see," he finally spoke.

"Jace'el." His name felt heavy and awkward on my tongue. "How can you look so human?"

In an infinite universe, I would have expected aliens to look vastly different.

"We spent two years in our chamber pods adapting to your earthen environment. Our bodies have changed to mimic the most efficient and dominant life form on the planet. Our ship took data from the environment and fed it to us. That is also how we have come to know your language. We still bare the marks of other worlds," he said, and pulled down the collar of his jacket to reveal three long, scar-like marks on each side of his neck. They looked like they had once been gills.

"What is your real form?" Though I asked the question, I wasn't sure I wanted the answer. After all, his real body might be the stuff of nightmares. Then it would have probably ruined the memory of the night.

"We no longer know our true forms."

"How many planets have you been to?" My heart pummeled against my ribs. If they'd gone to so many different worlds and moved on in one lifetime, what were they doing that would cause them to leave?

"Not all have been as receptive as yours. Then there are those that could not have sustained life had we stayed. If a planet cannot survive with our presence, we do not stay."

For every answer I was getting, more questions sprang up in my mind. "But why did you leave your planet? Are you explorers?"

He tilted his head, eyebrows drawn. "Did you not listen to the talks tonight?"

I bit down on my lip, knowing full well I hadn't. I had been too distracted. Hesitantly, I shook my head. "No," I admitted.

"The star of Vor'on died."

"Vor'on is your world?"

"Yes. Most Vor'onins did not make it off the surface in time."

The slit pupils of his eyes narrowed as he dropped his gaze.

My heart squeezed at the thought of losing most of the human population. It had probably felt like endless searching for a new home after such a horrible tragedy. I never expected such a heart breaking explanation.

"I'm so sorry," I whispered, placing a hand on his arm as I took a step closer. Our bodies were a hair's breadth away from touching. As much as I wanted to comfort him, I didn't know if he would find a hug comforting, or confusing.

I dropped my chin, regretting having brought the subject up. My curiosity had turned cruel.

Jace'el's hand brushed a strand of hair off his forehead. I looked up to find him smiling down at me. The moment I looked into his eyes, the heat that had filled me earlier, returned and all thoughts of sadness, vanished.

I don't know if it was my doing or his, but I was possessed by the desire to be as close to him as physically possible. I angled my face, pushing up on my toes, as he leaned closer until our lips brushed with the softest touch.

His hands cupped my face as he deepened the kiss. The touch of his mouth on mine sent electricity through my body, making every nerve sing.

The kiss grew deeper, and his hands shifted. One slid down my back, pressing me tighter against him, as the other tangled in my hair.

His teeth lightly grazed my bottom lip, drawing a moan from

deep inside my chest. I gripped the sleeves of his jacket until my fingers ached, pulling him closer, trying to meld our bodies into a single form.

My legs weakened and gave out. Jace'el gently lowered us until we were kneeling. It lasted only a brief moment, but it could have been a lifetime.

Eventually, I pulled away, nearly panting. The world around me grew hazy, and he was all I could see. I pressed my fingertips to my lips, swollen from our kiss.

"Why do I feel like this around you?" I managed to ask though a dry throat.

"I don't know. We do not do this on Vor'on."

"You don't kiss?"

He shook his head, resting his forehead against mine.

"Then, what do you do to show attraction?"

"We do not have such a thing. It could lead to the wrong pairing."

I was taken aback. "But what about love?"

"Love?"

I hesitated, not sure how to explain such a concept to someone who didn't know.

"Well," I began slowly. "Being in love is like —" I stopped.

The sound of a door opening, from down the hall, broke through the silence of the house. I listened intently as the sound of footsteps walked closer, pausing outside my door. I held my breath for a long moment, waiting for them to continue walking, afraid to move or make a sound.

A long, painful moment later, whichever family member it was, had left. That had been too close.

"You should go," I hated saying it, but I had crossed so many lines tonight already, I didn't want to continue to push my luck. "Will you meet me in the park tomorrow?"

"Yes."

A door closed and the sound of water running met my ears through the wall. It was now, or risk being caught.

I led him to the window and held aside my curtains as he climbed out. He reached for a branch, and I stopped him, my hand on his wrist. Jace'el turned back to me. I leaned forward and pressed my mouth against his one last time. My doorknob turned and clicked, creaking as it opened.

We pulled apart, my heart pounding with adrenaline.

"Go," I whispered. But he was already halfway down.

Spinning, I saw my mother standing in the doorway.

Chapter Eight

The First

I rubbed my eyes, squinting into the morning sun. I'd pressed my luck last night. Mom had come to check on me just as Jace'el had left. Luckily, when I'd told her I couldn't sleep, she'd been too tired to notice I'd been lying. Or maybe there had been enough honesty to my words that they'd rang true on some level.

I don't think I'd have been asleep at that moment even without my visitor. As it was, I had barely managed to fall asleep an hour or so before sunrise.

My fingers touched my lips as I closed my eyes once more, remembering the feel of Jace'el. The excitement of meeting him today made my heart beat faster, fully waking me.

I sprang out of bed and went downstairs. The local news was playing low on the T.V. as I made my way to the kitchen. Everyone was already dressed and finished with breakfast when

I entered.

Mom was at the table doing the crossword, and Dad was at the sink washing the breakfast dishes.

Toby's eyebrows shot up. "You slept in late."

The tone of his voice irked me, even if it was only noticeable to me because he knew I'd snuck out.

"Are you feeling better this morning?" Mom asked.

"Yeah, like new." I smiled and walked to the cupboard to grab the cereal and a bowl.

"So, Ray-Ray, what are your plans for the day?" she asked as I reached in the fridge to get the milk.

"I thought I'd go to the park today, maybe walk around town."

"Hot date?" Toby asked snidely, smirking at me.

I shot a glare in his direction. "No, I just want to enjoy my weekend outside before I go back to school tomorrow. Not everyone likes to stay inside all the time."

"I want you home before dark. It's a school night," Dad interjected as I plopped down at the table and began spooning bites of cereal into my mouth.

The past few weeks, he'd grown so over-protective. I knew he was just stressed about the Others since the situation was still so new. We really didn't know much about them. But hadn't they proved they meant to blend in and help? They'd nearly wiped out starvation and solved so many of the problems our world had been struggling with throughout history. Our world was turning into a utopia. Something that should have been impossible.

"You're not choking, are you?" Toby snapped me out of my reverie.

I nearly spit my food out as I tried to talk and swallow at the same time, earning obnoxious laughter as he left the room.

I hurriedly finished and excused myself, eager to get ready.

"*All anti-weapon borders have been resurrected as of yesterday,*" a reporter was saying. I stopped in my tracks and watched the news story while leaning on the back of the couch. "*The bill to disarm nuclear weapons passed by eighty-one percent early this morning despite protests of those against.*"

My jaw dropped open. I had expected all of this to take months, even years. But everything was moving fast. Though, who was I to say what had happened during official meetings. With our overly cautious government, who knew what the process, or number of sleepless nights even, had been to get to this point.

As interested as I was in this, I had an alien I wanted to meet. I rushed upstairs and got dressed.

An hour later, I was leaning against an oak tree in the park. Jace'el was nowhere to be seen. The ship that had sat in the far side had moved to one of the sanctioned grounds the government had created for them.

A hand fell onto my shoulder, making me jump. I spun and came face to face with a broad chest.

"Jace," I said. "You scared me."

"You said to meet you here. Is this not what you meant?"

"Yes, it is."

"You called me Jace. My name is Jace'el."

I blinked, then felt the warmth of a blush heat my cheeks. "Sorry, it's just easier for me to say. I won't do it again."

"No, I like it." He gave an uncertain smile.

"I thought we could walk around. I could show you the city."

"I would like that."

We started walking and crossed a good part of the city before I noticed some people were giving us looks. As accepting as this city was, I think there was a limit to how quickly something new was thought of as okay. The eyes that followed us made me nervous, distracting me from our time together.

"Let's go somewhere we can talk," I suggested, unable to take the stinging tension any longer.

"Where would you like to go?" he asked. His gaze darted around at the people passing us, giving us strange looks. It seemed like he'd also noticed the change of atmosphere.

We walked silently to the light rail, and rode it to the edge of the city near the zoo. Stepping out on the Washington Street platform, the fresh air was relieving after being cooped up in a small space with several people coughing and sneezing.

"My ship is near here," Jace pointed out.

My eyes widened. I wondered if anyone had been inside their ships yet, and if not, I could help hoping to be one of the first.

"Can we go see it?"

There was a hesitation before he responded, "Yes."

I could hardly hold my excitement in. Weaving my fingers

through his, I walked leaning into his side. It was nice to be able to walk the short distance with him. There was hardly anyone else around.

Jace led the way, stopping at the edge of the Washington Street Park. I looked away from his face to the once open space.

My jaw dropped.

Spread out before us were dozens of shining ships.

I dropped his hand and walked forward. He didn't make any noise, but I knew he followed close behind as I wove in and out from between the ships.

"Mine is over there," Jace said, pointing to one a few rows away.

It perched in the center of the park and was slightly larger than the others. I turned to him. "Who *are* you?"

He took a step toward me with an uncertain smile playing on his lips. "I am Jace'el."

"No, I mean, you were next to Thral'el the day you all left your ships, and yours is the largest one here. Are you one of the leaders?"

Jace started walking toward the center. "I have no power within the house yet. Thral'el is my father."

"Can we go inside?"

He turned sharply, his eyes clouded over. "No, that is not a good idea."

I was disappointed, but I'd wanted to spend the day with him. Walking around and looking at the ships was just extra. I wanted to talk with him, know who Jace'el was, and why he'd captured my every thought.

"That's okay. Maybe we can sit under the tree over there and talk? There's still so much I want to know about you."

His expression cleared. "Yes, you still haven't explained *love*."

I laughed, remembering our interrupted conversation from the night before.

We settled on the grass laying side by side, looking up at the clouds. Jace turned his head toward me and gave me a crooked smile, exposing one canine slightly more elongated than my own. I marveled at the similarities and differences between us. It was easy to forget he wasn't human.

The way I felt near Jace was unreal. The proximity of him was a drug that called to my body.

Turning to my side, I propped my head on my hand and looked at him. "Last night you said that the Vor'onins," I hesitated at the word, wondering if I'd said it correctly. When he didn't correct me, I continued, "don't have attraction. How do you continue your race? What if you end up stuck with someone you hate?"

I wasn't sure if it was an invasion of some kind, but I wanted to understand him better. I wanted to understand why I was so intensely drawn to him in every way, and why he seemed to respond in kind. And I trusted he would be forward enough to tell me if I crossed any lines.

"We are paired by the elder council based on leadership alliance as well as genetic compatibility to produce the best offspring."

"That sounds awful," I managed to say.

Jace turned to me. "The strongest and most intelligent offspring have the best chance at survival."

"I understand that." I reached out, placing my hand on top of his. "But I can't imagine being with someone I wasn't in love with, or at least attracted to."

"We didn't have these complications on Vor'on." His golden, amber eyes raked over my body. My face warmed, and I could almost feel the sensation of his hands on my skin.

"I don't understand." I pulled my hand away and averted my eyes, studying the blades of grass that poked out from between my fingers. "I thought you felt the same way I do. I feel like something is pushing me to be closer to you. I don't know how to explain it."

The turn of the conversation made me uncomfortable. I pushed myself up to sit, folding my legs under me. Jace sat up and moved a hand toward mine, but kept a small space between us.

"I feel that too," his voice was so quiet, I almost didn't hear over the rushing of my own blood through my veins.

"What?" I asked. My jaw went slack. "But you said —"

"Before you ran into me, I've never felt like this."

"Ran into you?" I jerked my chin up to meet his gaze. It took me a minute to realize he meant during the dance. My fingers flew to my mouth. "Oh…"

We stayed quiet, trying to understand what was happening

between us.

"You never told me what *love* is," he said after a long moment.

I swallowed thickly. "It's a feeling, like attraction, but deeper. Attraction is the physical part of it. Love is the emotional aspect." I cleared my throat. "With love, you want to be with someone no matter what life throws at you. You want to protect someone, and want the best for them—even if it means that you have to sacrifice your own safety, or something that would benefit you. It's a force you can't see, touch, or control. You just *feel* it inside."

It was an inadequate explanation. There were too many types and variables to be able to explain to someone who hadn't grown up feeling it.

Jace's eyes clouded over as he sat deep in thought. I couldn't imagine how overwhelming it was for him to try to understand concepts he had never experienced before.

I leaned my head back and looked at the pink and orange tinted clouds moving lazily across the pale blue sky.

"I find myself never wanting to leave your side. I can't seem to avoid the power that compels me toward you," he said drawing my attention back to him.

He leaned forward, cupping my cheek with a hand, and guided my face closer to his. I licked my lips. My eyelids slid shut as my body anticipated the weight of his kiss.

Jace was stiff, and despite being graceful in his every movement, awkward. He hardly spoke, usually only answering questions I'd asked. But when we touched, it seemed like the most natural thing in the world. It made everything else around us seem forced and strange.

A vibration in my back pocket made me jump, startling me from the moment. I licked my lips and pulled out my phone.

Dad's pissed. Where are you?

Crap, I thought. I hadn't realized how late it had gotten. Looking back at Jace, I knew I had only two options. I could stay out late to spend time with him and then lose my freedom for the next year. Or, I could force myself to go and see him again tomorrow. My heart protested, saying it was an impossible choice.

"I have to go," I managed to say. I stood, placing my phone back.

"Will I see you tomorrow?" Jace asked as he stood with me.

I fidgeted. "I have school tomorrow, but after that I can see you."

"I will see you then." Jace stepped forward and pulled me close.

His lips pressed against mine, the touch set every inch of my skin singing. Our kiss grew more passionate as he pressed me tighter. His lips moved down along my jaw, making me breathless. My thoughts spun out of control, growing hazy.

Another buzz from my phone had me pulling back, panting for breath.

My fingers tightened on the cloth of his shirt as my body fought itself, wanting nothing more than to crush myself against him.

Reluctantly, I relinquished my hold and flexed my aching joints. As if sensing my inner war, or perhaps waging one of his own, Jace took a step back. I hesitated a moment longer before I forced my feet to turn and head back toward the light rail station.

I moved as if I walked on air, though my heart was heavy. Inside, I felt different, as if I were changing. I didn't understand how, but I knew it was because of him.

With one look and one touch, I had gone to a place I could not return from, even if I'd wanted to.

I stood at the elevator entrance that led to the underground platform.

"Come on," I grumbled. Pressing the down button several more times, I could hardly contain the anxiety that filled me. It wouldn't do any good, but I was eager to get home before the sun set.

The steel doors opened and a few people filed out. I moved to enter and a man forcing his way into the elevator nearly jostled me into the wall, trying to get into the elevator before me. I narrowed my eyes, expecting an apology at least, but he just stood in the corner, staring blankly ahead. His face was a sickly pale color, almost greenish.

I let the matter go, seeing how sick he was, and stepped in, doing my best to breathe as shallowly as I could. There were only two buttons on the panel. One labeled 'the present,' and the other that would lead to the track level labeled 'sixteen million years ago'—the city's attempt at geological humor. I pressed the button for the bottom level.

The elevator opened to a tunnel full of people. It was strange to see it so busy at this time of day. I made my way through the crowd as the train approached. It screeched to a halt, sparks flickering as metal scratched against metal.

People shoved their way onto the car. I was pushed back and forth between them like a rag doll. Just one of the down sides to being shorter than most people.

There was a commotion at the far end of the tunnel, but it hardly registered. My mind had snapped back to Jace like a rubber band as soon as I'd stood still. I missed him. It had only been minutes, but it didn't seem to matter.

I pressed my hand to my forehead. It wasn't hot. I wasn't sick, so that wasn't the reason I seemed to be so attached to a man I'd just met. It had been less than twenty-four hours, and if it had been any significant amount of time, I would have sworn I'd developed deep feelings for him.

Was that possible? I wondered. Jace might look like a human in many ways, but he wasn't. He was an alien, with different biology. It felt as though I had to keep reminding myself of that fact. How could I have fallen for someone so impossibly fast?

I finally managed to make my way onto the train when a bone-chilling scream filled the air. I froze and turned, straining my neck to see what had happened, but I couldn't see past the sea of people crammed around me.

The few people, who hadn't made it onto one of the cars before the doors closed, scattered.

Except for the man from the elevator.

He ran toward my car, not slowing as he approached. My eyes widened, and I took a half a step back. He was going to —

The man slammed into the car. His fingers pried at the doors to no avail. Unseeing eyes seemed to stare inside, searching for something, or someone. His hands pawed at the windows as the light rail started to move. Bloodied fingers left trails of red streaking across the glass.

Chapter Nine

Borders

Red smeared against black, filling the edges of my vision. Eyes, made pale blue by clouds, pierced the darkness, targeting me and rooting my feet to the ground. I couldn't escape it, my body refused to fight the fear that held me captive. Then an ear-splitting scream sounded again, filling my head. My hand shot to the side of my head with a hard clap.

I sat up gasping and holding my head. My tank top was drenched with sweat. I blinked and tried to shake out the ringing in my ears.

It was only a dream.

Reaching toward my nightstand, I turned off the alarm that had been the scream in my dream. I couldn't get the image of the man out of my head. Through the night, my mind had warped what happened in the tunnel into something out of a horror movie.

My head pounded, and I felt as though I hadn't slept at all. I threw my blankets off me and made my way to the shower, dying to wash away the images that haunted me all night.

I turned the faucet and stripped as steam filled the room. Stepping under the water, I bowed my head and let the heat flow over every inch of me. My body ached with exhaustion, and I hoped the day would go by fast.

The bell rang and a jolt of adrenaline snapped my eyes open. My chin slid off my hand and jerked upright. I let out a groan. I'd been fighting all day to keep from falling asleep in class, and failing. Miranda had been in most of my classes and kept nudging me awake.

By the time I stood to gather my things, the room was already nearly empty. Only Miranda had stayed back to wait.

"Ray, what's with you? You've been out of it all day." Her dark eyes filled with concern as she studied my face.

"I didn't sleep well, that's all," I admitted. I didn't want to go into detail about it. No part of me wanted to relive that horrible nightmare.

"Well, wake up. Mr. Bellevue assigned us a butt load of work for our first day back and it's all due this Friday. Do you want to come over to my house and study? We could get it done faster."

I was just about to accept her invitation when I remembered Jace said he would meet me after school. "I can't, I made plans yesterday."

"Plans? With who? You never make plans with anyone but me." She crossed her arms and looked at me as if trying to read my mind. Miranda knew me better than anyone, but even she wouldn't be able to guess this time.

"Oh, it's nothing. You don't know him." I waved her off, hoping she'd drop it.

Miranda's hand whipped out and grabbed my arm, pulling me to a stop.

"Excuse me?" A knowing grin formed on her lips. I'd slipped up and she caught the detail I hadn't meant to share. "Who is this guy, and how long have you been hiding him from me?"

My face flushed. My sluggish mind had let me say too much. "Uh… well… he… uh…" I stammered. "I met him at the ball."

Confusion crossed her face, then understanding. "Oh, Josh! I didn't think he was your type, but it's about time you gave someone a chance, Ray."

"No, it's not Josh," I said, lowering my voice. My cheeks burned hotter.

We walked down the hall, already deserted by students eager to get home.

"What do you mean? I didn't see you with anyone else. If it's not Josh…"

I couldn't take the interrogation. I was too sleep deprived to think clearly. Sharing anything about Jace wasn't something I'd planned on doing, not for a while anyway. But I'd already said too much to take back.

We pushed through the building's side doors, which led to the parking lot.

He could have been waiting on anyone as he stood casually leaning against a tree, legs crossed and hands shoved in the pockets of his pants. Anyone else would have mistaken him for just another student. But his golden amber eyes shone up at me.

"Ray?" Miranda frowned back at me from the bottom of the steps.

I'd stopped in my tracks the second I'd seen Jace waiting for me, but she'd kept walking. She jogged back up to where I stood and looked between Jace and me.

"Do you know him?"

My tongue darted out between my suddenly parched lips. Jace straightened and took a few steps toward me. I forced myself to face my friend.

"Yeah." I barely managed to get the word out.

"Is that the guy?" She leaned in and whispered.

I nodded.

At seeing my hesitation and Miranda's stare, Jace stopped walking. Before I knew what was happening, she spun me around, and dragged me back inside.

"Ray, are you kidding me? You made plans with an *alien*?"

She glanced out the window. "You did know he was one of the Others, right?"

I ran my fingers through my hair, trying unsuccessfully to avoid her gaze. Releasing a sigh, I let my hand fall to my side and shrugged. "Yeah, I knew."

"Then what are you doing with him?" Her harsh tone was unexpected.

"Wasn't it your idea to go to the ball and meet them?" I asked a little more defensively than I'd meant to.

"Yeah, but not get one to follow you around like a puppy. Do you know what your parents would do? How the school would react if they knew?"

I took a step back. "Miranda, they are going to this school so we can get to know them. Why shouldn't we even try?"

"Because I saw the look on your face when you said you'd made plans." She straightened her posture. "This means more to you than just getting to know him."

"It's fine, I promise. He won't hurt me, he's a nice guy." I moved to go out the door.

"Ray, we don't know anything about them. What if he gets mad and eats your face?"

I laughed. "I highly doubt that would happen."

"How can you be so sure?" she drilled. Her hands rested on her hips.

"Miranda, I doubt the government would allow them to integrate if they had a habit of eating faces."

"Fine, but will you at least text me when you get home?"

"Promise," I said, crossing my finger over my heart in an X motion.

"If you die, can I have your computer?" she called after me.

"Deal," I said. I pushed open the door and walked toward Jace, my heart hammering against my ribcage.

Three hours later, I was walking home from the park with a large smile on my face. The sound of sirens a few miles away blended in with the other city noises, but I'd hardly noticed.

I stepped over the threshold of my house to find my dad pacing back and forth. He stopped and narrowed his eyes at me, fists clenched.

"Where have you been?" he spoke through gritted teeth.

"I was just out," I said, taken aback. It wasn't unusual for me to go to a friend's place after school.

"I've been calling you for hours. Why didn't you pick up?"

Reaching in my pocket, I grabbed for my phone and looked at the display. "Sorry, it must have died without me realizing it." I spoke slowly, unsure if I would make his anger worse. "What's wrong?"

"I want you to come straight home after school from now on."

"What? Why?" I could feel the blood drain from my face.

There was no way I was in that much trouble for not coming straight home.

My eyes flicked upstairs, unsure if Toby had told them about me sneaking out two nights ago. I set my mouth in a tight line.

"I want to know you're safe."

"Safe from what?"

Getting him to tell me what was happening was like pulling teeth. It was as if he was avoiding the real problem, whatever that was.

"From the Others," he stated simply.

"They are becoming part of our society. I can't avoid them unless you lock me in my room."

He glowered as if he was actually considering it. We were both usually even tempered, but when we butted heads, there was a tendency for our arguments to get heated fast, and spin out of control. I was always on the losing side.

After several moments, I realized fighting him on this wouldn't get us anywhere. I took several slow, deep breaths and eventually my body let go of the tension. "I'm sorry. I didn't mean to make you worry."

"It's okay, Ray," my dad said, dismissing me.

I trudged up to my room. I dropped my bag at the foot of my bed, falling face first into the mattress, and letting my body bounce limply atop the covers. Rolling over, I stared at the ceiling.

I looked to the window as I sat up. We had to find a way

around this new fear. It had only been a few days, and I knew I couldn't give him up. There was still so much I wanted to know about him. The way he made me feel was so much better than any book or movie could ever promise.

An idea formed in my mind. I had to talk to Jace tonight.

It was a risk. There was a chance I'd get caught, but I didn't care. Thankfully, I'd already missed dinner so the chances of someone coming to my room were lower. I opened my window, reached for a thick branch to steady myself, and climbed down.

I landed in a crouch and looked around before standing. The coast was clear. My dad wouldn't be coming for hours to check on me, if at all. He always gave me time to cool off after a fight before we talked again. I took off running, not slowing until I was a block away. I panted, trying to catch my breath as I attempted to work out the stitch in my side while walking.

I made my way to the bus stop. The idea of giving the light rail another chance so soon sent shivers down my spine. Especially after the nightmare it gave me last time.

This time of day, the bus was mostly empty. No crowds to contend with. The windows of the city skyline reflected the fading light of the sun. It was almost as if the city belonged to me alone.

The ride to Washington Street Park was slower this way, but the bus still made good time. I stepped out onto the curb and glanced around. There was hardly anyone out. A chill crawled over my skin. I rubbed my arms, wishing I'd remembered to bring a light jacket with me.

I scanned the ships in the park and tried to remember which one was Jace's, but in the dimming light, they all looked exactly the same. Over a dozen silhouettes were spread out across the park, changing the tranquil landscape to an otherworldly phenomenon. I wandered around the edge of the park, trying to find the spot we'd stopped at the day before.

A man ambled down the street toward me, swaying with every step. He looked drunk. There was something unsettling about the way his gaze locked on me. I'd wished I had a reason to cross the street to give myself more space, but this is where I needed to be.

Instead, I turned, cutting across the grass, and headed toward the ships. Nervously looking over my shoulder, I saw the man had also changed directions, unmistakably coming at me from an angle. My throat dried when I realized he'd started running. There was nothing subtle about his dark intentions. They would lead to pain or murder, maybe both. Sneaking out had been a bad idea.

My legs shook as he sped up.

I needed help. I needed to get to Jace.

I had no idea why this psycho was after me, or what he wanted, but I was not interested in finding out.

I ran as hard as I could. All the running I've ever done did little to help me. My lungs struggled to pull in oxygen; my breathing was erratic from adrenaline laced with fear.

A low growl from behind spurred me on through the pain of my burning muscles.

Chancing a glance over my shoulder, my feet slipped on the damp grass. I felt myself lose traction, and I fell. I crashed hard on the ground, landing on my stomach. I looked back. He was still coming.

Rage distorted his face, and large patches of some dark substance stained his clothes. His speed was unreal. He barreled down at me like a freight train. By the time I would have managed to stand, he would have been on top of me.

Uselessly, I tried to scramble away. The pounding of my attacker's footsteps drew nearer. My heart pummeled against my sternum, deafening me. He lunged, and I screamed.

I raised my arms to shield my eyes, not wanting to see the horrifying look of insanity. Tensing, I braced for impact.

CHAPTER TEN

Curfew

There was a grunt, a flash of light, then the sound of a body hitting the ground. I whipped my head up to see what had happened. My heart was still beating frantically, drowning out the rest of the world with its pounding.

Jace stood over the man's still form, his fists clenched at his sides. He bent down, his body blocking my view. I heard a soft snap.

He stood and faced me. Worry was etched in the draw of his eyebrows.

I could hardly breathe, and for the first time, I felt the tears that streamed down my face. Grateful didn't even begin to explain how I felt. My sobs increased as they turned from ones of fear, to ones of relief.

"Are you okay?" Jace asked, kneeling beside me. He pulled me into his arms. I held on to him with all the strength my arms could muster.

I shook my head and held tightly to Jace as if he were my lifeline. And in this case, I suppose he had been.

"Wh-what was that?" I asked between sniffles. "Why did he come after me?"

There was a long pause as I waited for him to explain.

"I don't know," he said finally.

"Is-is he dead?" It was impossible to speak without stuttering between sniffles.

"Yes." His voice was low and full of uncertainty.

"What did you do to him?" I pulled back to look into his eyes. His expanding pupils had nearly swallowed his beautiful irises, leaving just a thin golden ring around the darkness.

"I marked him for retrieval for study. Someone will come for him soon."

I let my grip loosen. Drying my eyes with my sleeve, I frowned. "Why would you need to study him? Was he human or Vor'onin?"

"There was something wrong with his cells that our ships did not sense during our stasis. We do not take chances with potential biological threats." He only half answered my question. I assumed he wasn't sure. But then why would his people pick up dead humans? It was probably one of them.

When I was finally calm enough to stand, Jace lent his arm to steady me.

"Thank you for saving me," I mumbled and took a few steps away from the dead man, refusing to look.

"What were you doing out here? We weren't supposed to meet until tomorrow." He brushed my hair out of my face. His hands cupped my cheeks as his eyes scanned over my body, looking for injuries.

"I'm fine." I pushed his hands down and pushing myself up on my toes, I wrapped my arms around his neck and lowered his head, pressing my lips against his in a brief kiss.

"Raylinn," he whispered my name, though it sounded stilted as his tongue stumbled over the unfamiliar syllables. His speech was spot on with most words, but he had trouble with names.

I'd almost forgotten the reason I came. After the attack, it seemed to be a minor issue. I realized I'd overreacted to my dad's proclamation. But then, it seemed I didn't always think clearly with Jace involved. I could have spoken to Jace after school the next day. It would have only taken a few moments.

"I can't meet you after school tomorrow; I have to go home right away."

His posture lost some of its strength. "Did I do something wrong?"

"No," I said louder than necessary. "No. It's just a rule my dad made today. He doesn't trust your people."

"What about you, do *you* trust us?"

The hurt in his voice almost broke me. "I trust *you*, Jace."

He slipped his hands out of mine and ran his fingers up my arm.

"Let me take you home," he said. His eyes dropped to the body off to the side. "I don't want you wandering out here alone."

Jace escorted me all the way home. The bus ride was silent and we hardly spoke on our walk, but he never once let go of my hand until we stood against the tree outside my room. I felt safe with him at my side.

It was then that he let go of me. He had a hard time meeting my gaze and started to turn away. I reached out and guided his face toward me until he finally looked at me.

"What's wrong?" I asked.

"I am afraid I will not see you again. I don't want that."

Jace felt the same!

My heart both soared and squeezed painfully at the same time. Whatever was going on between us, it wasn't stronger on my end—a secret fear I'd had, but refused to admit to myself, or even think about.

"Jace," I began. "This is really fast, and it makes no sense, but I don't want that to happen either."

Tension melted from his shoulders, and he stepped closer. Jace placed his hand on the back of my neck and lowered his face, stopping inches away. His other hand wrapped around my waist and rested on my lower back.

"There is nothing comparable to this on Vor'on. I don't understand this feeling. I would do anything, travel to the ends of the universe, if I had to, if it meant keeping you safe."

It was so easy for me to get lost in him. The way he looked at me, the scent of him, the caresses, the very way he held himself—everything called to my soul as if he were made for me, and me alone.

"I don't want to lose you," I said.

"I will never let that happen," he promised, closing the small distance between us.

Our kiss spoke of pledges made, and were solidified with every press of our fingers against each other's flesh, even above our clothing. It spoke of our determination not to lose each other, it spoke of something so much more than we could ever hope to express.

Eventually we pulled apart, just enough to speak. My fingers still gripped tightly to his shirt, keeping him close. My eyes remained closed, savoring the echoes of electricity his touch had left, making the nerves under my skin come alive and dance in anticipation.

"I never want to be apart from you," I whispered.

"Then I will stay by your side until you send me away. Not even death would keep me from you," he said, his voice hoarse. His heated words were enough to steal my breath, and I smiled knowing it would be the same for me.

Jace pulled back. "You should get inside, your skin feels chilled."

He was rubbing my arms softly. I hadn't noticed how cold it became after the sun had set.

I climbed the tree and pulled myself through the window. My body was sore from using muscles that hadn't been used in a while. I stretched my arms out to the side, pleasantly surprised when Jace wrapped his arms around my waist and turned me to face him.

He lifted my chin with a knuckle, and lowered his mouth to mine. I let myself melt into the safety of his arms.

"Goodnight, Raylinn," he whispered against my lips, and I could feel his words vibrate across the delicate skin.

His fingers lightly grazed against my neck and down over my shoulders and arms as he started to pull away. The lightest of touches left a trail of fire igniting all of my senses.

The words filled me with a clashing of fire and ice filled passion. Passion at the unspoken feelings behind his soft words, and anxiety for the unexpected fear of being alone.

"Don't leave," I pleaded, gripping him tighter to me.

If he left, I knew the nightmare from the other night would return, but this time, I knew it would be worse. The man from the park had the same look on his face as the first man who'd kept me from sleep the night before. I couldn't face another night of that, not when something this wonderful was within reach. The contrast would be too harsh.

Jace stiffened, then relaxed. "Yes."

Outside of this room, the rest of the world ceased to exist. All that remained was the two of us in this perfect moment that I wanted to last forever.

Jace was taller than I was, but our bodies fit perfectly

together. As we kissed, we moved toward the bed, collapsing on top of it. He placed kisses along my jaw and down my neck. My pulse jumped, and I felt it thunder against each brush of his lips.

His fingers danced along my skin as if he were trying to learn every inch of me. I tangled my fingers in his hair, trying to feel each kiss more than the last. Almost from the moment we'd met, he'd become my oxygen, and I his gravity.

I tore down the barrier that kept me from him since the moment we met and held nothing back. The fire that had been burning under it all was finally free to consume us from the inside out.

Eventually, with our limbs tangled together, we laid breathless, still holding tightly to the other. My eyes grew heavy and the call of sleep finally pulled me under where no nightmares could take hold, so long as Jace was with me.

Morning came too soon, and with it, the bight rays of sun streamed through the open window. I squeezed my eyes tighter and buried my face into Jace's bare chest. Birds chirped, lulling me into the delicious place between dreaming and waking. I listened to the soft pounding of his heart beating to its own unique rhythm, both similar to mine, but different.

A knock on my door roused me. I wanted to continue to sleep, basking in the feel of his body against mine. To ignore whoever was calling me back to the reality I wasn't yet ready to face again.

The knock came again, and this time my eyes flew open as I remembered myself. I pushed myself up and looked down at Jace's face. A peaceful smile rested on his lips as he slowly blinked awake.

"R—" he started, but I pressed a finger to his lips to keep him quiet.

I was dizzy with panic.

"Ray?" my dad's voice asked from the other side of the door. There was something about his tone I didn't like.

"Just a moment," I called. I jumped up and pulled Jace by the arm toward my closet. I pushed him inside, shoving his clothes with him and motioning him to stay quiet as I closed the shuttered doors.

Quickly, I slipped on my tank top and shorts that I had left lying on the carpet. I walked to the door and opened it just wide enough to stick out my head.

"What's up?" I asked, fighting the flush racing up my chest.

"I know you're getting ready for school, but I need to tell you something," he said. "May I come in?"

"What is it?" I asked suddenly worried. I stepped aside and let him through.

Dad walked in and sat down at my desk. "The government has instated a curfew."

"What? Why would they do that?" My jaw dropped. I was not thrilled with the idea of a police state in my city.

"There is a highly contagious virus going around, Ray," he

said. "Everyone is required to go straight to and from work or school, and then straight home. They're trying to limit exposure to the virus."

"That's insane!" my mind fought to make sense of it through the remaining hazy remnants of sleep. A chill ran up my spine, and I shivered. There was always a new disease being discovered, what made this one so different? "Why?"

Dad hesitated a moment before answering, then recited the facts, "The CDC hasn't released specifics yet, but they said people have already started dying. The incubation period is roughly twenty-four to fourth-eight hours from the first symptom. There have been a few cases of it even causing insanity and uncharacteristic violence in some people. Anyone showing any symptoms have been ordered to stay home and call a doctor immediately."

My jaw hung open in disbelief. I sat speechless, trying to process the news.

Dad stood, walked over to me, and placed a kiss on my forehead. "Be careful when you go out, there's already been several attacks. I don't want you catching whatever this is. I'll let you finish getting ready."

I nodded numbly. He seemed to be holding back, as if there was more to it then he was letting on, but he left the room, letting me know the conversation was over.

The curfew was too sudden. The government never reacted this fast to an illness. I couldn't remember ever hearing about one because of a disease. In fact, it was usually the opposite, so the one-eighty in attitude scared me.

I swallowed thickly. Wondering if anyone was afraid that it had to do with the Vor'onins, but that seemed too convenient. The Others were an easy scapegoat for whatever was developing. But then there was the possibility this virus was a direct result of them being here.

If it got out of hand, it could end up tearing Jace away from me. It was selfish, and I knew it, but the massive scale of the implications was too much, and I had to focus on the one thing my brain was able to easily process.

I felt my heart sink in my chest as it filled with cold shards of dread, and it was almost as if I were frozen in place, unable to move, while the world around me crumbled to ash.

CHAPTER ELEVEN

Gone

The door clicked shut and Jace quietly stepped out of the closet once again fully clothed. We stood motionless across the room from each other. His eyes were wide in surprise, and I knew my expression mirrored his.

"What does this mean?" I whispered almost to myself. My stomach rolled. I felt sick.

Jace didn't move, only dropped his gaze to the floor.

"Jace?" I said his name as I took a tentative a step forward. I didn't want to ask, but I had to know. My hands trembled as I gathered my courage to speak the words aloud. My voice came out strained and rough. "It wasn't the Vor'onins… was it?"

His jaw ticked, but he still didn't answer. I felt my legs growing weak.

"Jace… please tell me," I begged.

"I don't know." He looked up, his uncertain expression from moments ago had transformed into a hardened one. "But I will find out."

"Ja—"

Jace closed the distance between us with two long strides. His hands tangled in my already messy hair, and he kissed me with determination. It wasn't the same gentleness he'd lavished upon me the previous night. And as much as I wanted to get lost in it, I couldn't help but feel there was a sense of finality to it.

"I told you, I won't let anything keep me from your side."

He let go abruptly then moved to the window. Sending one final glance my way before he descended down the tree, he said, "I will meet you the same time as yesterday."

I nodded.

The Vor'onins had come to earth with gifts and promises of world peace. Things we've been attempting and failing at for generations upon generations. A time without war was something that was once impossible. But they'd done it. All wars had ceased within days of the technology they'd given us. They had brought peace to this blue planet. Starvation and hunger had become a thing of the past.

So why, if they wanted to bring destruction on us and rid us of our world so they could have it, would they bring us a way to save ourselves? It didn't make sense.

Then a horrible thought hit me. *The government?*

They depended on war and an imbalance of power. The

economy was tied heavily to militaries across the globe. Would they be willing to sacrifice our lives for the sake of getting the people to demand we send the Others away? It was psychotic if it were true. But both theories were just as likely.

Lunch rolled around and in true late spring fashion, the sky was overcast. Heavy clouds hovered drizzling, creating a subdued feel. Small groups of students were scattered around the cafeteria. I've never heard the school so quiet before. It was as if the curfew had silenced our voices. Maybe it was the fear of what such extreme measures meant.

We had been sheltered our whole lives. All the danger had always been far enough away that it never felt real. For the first time, we were at risk in such a way that we couldn't avoid simply by going on with our lives as usual.

"It's freaky, isn't it?" Miranda asked.

I shook off my distraction and turned to her. "Yeah," I agreed.

A group of Vor'onins walked through the double doors and split up, going about the same routine as everyone else. The only thing that set them apart were their high-collared jackets, similar in style to the ones they wore at the ball, only styled in a more casual manner.

All eyes turned to them.

The harsh whispers of "*Others*" could be heard around the room. In an instant, the somber mood changed to one of hostility.

This was the first week of their integration into schools and work places. On their first day, they were supposed go to an orientation session. They must have finished early because no one expected to see them yet. The next step was to assign them classes. Though with their technology, I doubted they needed our schools.

I admired how they ignored the tension in the room and went along peacefully, doing their best to fit in. Though most students ignored them, a few welcomed them. I caught sight of Jace as he was grabbing a lunch. I hoped he would see me and come sit with us. I raised my hand to wave at him, but changed my mind and ran my fingers through my hair instead before looking back down at my food.

A few minutes later, loud voices drew my attention to the far side of the room. Josh stood among his group of friends. His fists clenched at his sides. One of his friends had their hands on his chest, holding him back. I followed his gaze.

He'd somehow narrowed in on Jace.

I watched as his friends talked to him, trying to calm him down, and though he stopped trying to advance, he was still noticeably on edge. Josh shrugged them off in a manner that insisted he was okay. It wasn't the carefree face I remembered from the ball. But instead, one marred by a scowl.

Josh walked past several of the Vor'onins and headed for the soda machine. I kept my eye on him. His posture was volatile. From where I stood, if Josh wanted to start something, there wasn't anything I could have done. And with the tension from the new curfew and the news of the virus, confrontation was the last thing we needed.

"I'm going to get a drink. Do you want one?" I asked Miranda. I got up and rounded the table, heading straight for Josh before she could respond.

I was almost within speaking distance of Josh when he swerved in his path, bumping into Jace hard. In slow motion, Jace's tray crashed to the ground, and I could feel the room turn their attention toward them.

It was obvious Josh had shoulder checked him on purpose, and everyone knew it. But no one said anything. The Vor'onins were always graceful. They never tripped or dropped anything. In fact, their ability to be so graceful had been the subject of many conversations around school since we had learned they would be coming to join us.

"Josh," I said, but he was already set on his actions.

"Watch where you're going, *freak.*" Josh snarled, shoving Jace.

I blanched.

Jace managed to catch himself, and he stood upright. He towered over Josh, but kept his facial features neutral. I had to do something. I ran between them, placing my hand on each of their chests, trying to create some much-needed space.

"Josh," I said, looking between them.

My gaze must have lingered on Jace longer than I realized because I went flying to the side. I felt myself falling. Only the cold, tiled floor caught me. My head snapped back and hit the ground. Pain laced its way through my skull, and for a second, my vision went spotty.

Jace's eyes flashed with fire when he saw me hit the ground. Josh moved toward him again. The second Josh's hands connected with his chest, Jace's hand came up and pushed him with almost no effort. Josh went flying backward several yards before skidding to a stop. There had been a small flash of light—a spark of… *something*.

Jace took two steps toward me and stopped when several more people came between us. I caught his eyes over the top of them and shook my head mouthing "No."

He stopped, and I released a sigh of relief. I knew he'd fight his way through them to get to me, but that would have only made things worse.

Within moments, teachers and staff were there pushing aside the wall of Josh's friends, who had formed a circle around us. The gym teacher headed over to Josh, who was just starting to sit up while rubbing his head.

"Raylinn," the school nurse said. "Are you hurt?"

"No," I said, letting her help me stand.

Two teachers were already escorting Jace away alongside the principal.

"What did he do to you?" Nurse Winston asked. But she wasn't looking at Josh; she was looking at Jace.

"Nothing," I snapped defensively. "Josh pushed him and when I tried to separate them, *Josh* pushed me down."

She pressed her lips into a tight line as if she didn't quite believe me. "Why would he push you?"

I barely managed to hold back an annoyed huff. "I don't know. All I saw was Josh bump into Jace on purpose, trying to start a fight."

"Who's Jace?" she asked.

I'd used his name, not even his name, but the shortened informal one I'd been using. No one else knew there was something between us.

"Uh, the *alien*," I cringed at the word. He wasn't an alien, or one of the *Others* to me, he was so much more.

"Regardless, we don't put up with fighting at this school. He will be expelled."

"What? Josh was the one who started it!" my mouth dropped open in shock.

"Josh will be punished as well, but that is not your concern. Now, if you're all right then I suggest you go finish your lunch, and then get to class." She turned and walked away, leaving me gaping after her.

Numbly, I walked back to where I'd left Miranda.

"Holy crap, Raylinn. Are you okay?"

I nodded. "Yeah, I'm fine…"

"That went from zero to a million in a second. Why would you get between them like that?"

"Things are stressful enough with the curfew and everything. Fighting with them isn't going to help the situation." I frowned, rubbing the back of my head where a decent sized knot was already forming.

"Ray," Miranda started hesitantly. "You need to be careful. I know you're friends with him, or whatever, but a lot of people don't want them here."

"That's stupid. They've already done so much for this world. All they want is a place to live."

"Yah, I know, but it's stuff like that," she said circling a finger in front of my face. "That will have people questioning your loyalty."

I snorted. "Loyalty? To who, *earth*?"

"To *humans*. You seriously haven't noticed how a lot of people are resistant to them living here?" Miranda scoffed. "Where have you been?"

"Apparently, I've missed a lot in the last few days," I mumbled. I needed to pay more attention. I might have something amazing with Jace, but I'd missed the way everyone had turned from excited to hesitant, or worse—aggressive toward the Vor'onins.

I waited for as long as I could after school, but Jace never showed. I wondered if the principal had told him to stay off school property, and instead he had waited across the street, but still, he never met me. I got a lot of strange looks for standing and waiting while everyone rushed to make it home. I barely made it home in time to avoid my parents questioning me.

Ever since lunch, there had been a dark cloud hovering over

me. I'd hoped Jace would stop by later. I ran upstairs and tried to work on homework, but after a few hours, I still couldn't focus. I couldn't keep my worry over Jace at bay. I moved to the bed and waited for a tap on my window, but instead, there was a knock at my door and Toby stuck his head in a second later.

"Can I come in?" he asked as he closed the door behind him, not waiting for an answer.

"What do you want?" I pushed myself up to sit, leaning back on my arms.

"I heard what happened at school today."

"It's fine, Toby," I said with an irritated groan. For the rest of the day, people were either worried about me, or gave me strange looks. Though I did suspect the worry people showed was more just their curiosity to be one of the first to know what had happened from the source.

"What were you thinking?" he asked, just like everyone else had.

"I was the closest one to them, and I just don't think fighting is going to help things," I said robotically.

"This wouldn't have to do with the way you've been acting since last Saturday, would it?"

"No," I said slowly. I eyed him suspiciously. *How much did he know?* I wondered.

"Whatever, Ray," he said, and I knew he didn't believe me by his tone, but he didn't press me any further. Toby stood and headed for the door.

"You're not going to tell Mom and Dad, are you?" I asked,

hating the pleading tone that snuck into my words.

"No," he said, not turning to face me as his hand rested on the doorknob. "They have enough to worry about. Just… be more careful, okay?"

"Okay, thank you," I said quietly as he walked out.

Jace never stopped by that night, or the following nights. That weekend, I paced like a tiger in a small cage around the house, spending most of my time in my room waiting for Jace to come. There were times I wondered if he was waiting for me near the park where all the ships were, but I figured if I didn't show up, he'd know to come here.

I spent all Sunday scared he was angry with me for not letting him come to me during that confrontation. But he was smart, and he would have known why I wouldn't let him. My thoughts ping-ponged back and forth like that for a week. Worry and hope… in an endless cycle.

Then weeks passed, and I could never seem to find an opportunity to go to him. Public transportation stopped. The more time that passed, the fewer and fewer Vor'onins there were at school, until they were just *gone*. No one spoke about why, there was no announcement, and everyone just seemed to act as if they had never been there.

I became listless in all aspects of my life, and everyone was noticing. My family seemed to assume it was because of the curfew. We were all acting irritable. It had been almost a month since the government had instated it.

And I still hadn't heard, or seen, anything from Jace. What

had happened to the promise he'd made?

I rolled over and faced the wall, holding a pillow to my chest while trying not to cry. I didn't want to get to that point. Part of me still held onto a small sliver of hope that I wasn't ready to give up.

My eyes just started to slide shut when a light tapping set my heart to racing. I didn't move as I waited to see if it was my imagination.

Tap, tap, tap.

There it was!

I sprung up from my bed and rushed to the window, pulling it open. There he was, as if it had only been a few hours.

"Jace," I said.

"May I come in?" he asked after a long moment.

The shock of finally seeing him had kept me rooted in place, and I'd been blocking his way in. I backed up, giving him room.

"What are you doing here? Why haven't you come by at all?" I questioned him. "I missed you…"

"I couldn't get here before now, but I need to talk to you," he said as he straightened.

The look on his face quailed the excitement and joy I'd felt at his presence.

He didn't wear the smile I'd expected to see stretched across his lips, and his sparkling eyes were dark.

I felt a pit form in my stomach at the foreboding tone of his voice.

Chapter Twelve

Truth

"What happened? Where have you been?" I asked.

"I was unable to get away before now," he said, as if that explained anything.

I waited for him to continue, but he didn't. I should have pressed him for answers, but I was so relieved to see him that I rushed into his arms instead. Immediately, the familiar scent of him filled my senses and a weight lifted off my chest. It had been slowly crushing me during his absence and I hadn't noticed until it was gone. In the same second he gathered me up into his arms.

"I wanted to come find you," I said, snuggling into him. "They stopped the busses and light rails. The highways have been shut down too, and with the curfew, I couldn't get out of the house."

Being in his arms, I realized I needed him. I needed him like I needed every breath and every beat of my heart. Somehow, he'd become the force that kept me alive.

"I know. They put up barricades around the city, dividing them into sectors."

Pulling back, I met his gaze. "What? They haven't said anything about that in the news. How can they do that without us knowing?"

I wondered how wrapped up in my own little world I'd been to not have noticed something so big.

"My guess is that they are trying to isolate the virus," he said, letting his voice trail off quietly.

"Or?" I asked. There was more to it than he was telling me.

"Or that they are trying to keep you from knowing the full extent of what's happening."

"But, they can't do that, the media would tell us." Unless they, too, were subjected to the barricades and were being fed stories. Thinking back over the recent news coverage I had seen, I realized they had all been within a studio, without the usual field reporters. All new information was read by a written memo.

Jace frowned. I believed him. Of course he would know, he'd just crossed the city to be with me. He wouldn't come all this way just to lie to me.

It had been so long since I'd last seen him. I missed being near him. Though as much as I wanted to lie down and wrap myself up in him again, I still had so many unanswered questions.

"Jace, where have you been? What happened that day at

school? I've never seen anything like that before."

A slight blush crept over his face as he looked away. "I didn't mean to do that. It's a defense mechanism, a bioelectric charge we emit when being attacked."

"I know Josh went too far, but I don't think he needed to be shocked like that."

His brows furrowed. "I don't control it. It's a response we are born with that our bodies give off to protect itself."

"It won't happen randomly when we touch, will it?" The thought of him not having any control of it made me uneasy.

"No, unless you tried to kill me, it would never happen."

I'd never seen him so uncomfortable. Guilt washed off him in waves so I let the subject drop. "Do you know where the virus came from?"

"No, but I want to talk to our anchorite, Char'ra. She might know how it can be stopped."

I wrinkled my nose. "Huh? Your who?"

"Char'ra is the anchorite of our house. She's like a … *sage*, that gives us council."

With him going back to his ship, it was the perfect opportunity to go with him. I could search for something, anything, to prove it wasn't the Vor'onins who'd released the virus. The fallout of my world even *thinking* it could be them would be disastrous.

"I'm coming with you," I said as I set my jaw with determination.

"No, Raylinn, it is too—"

"I'm not letting you do this alone," I insisted. He was hesitant to take me to his ship, but I was resolved to go aboard. This was too important, and I couldn't just sit back and let myself feel useless.

He took a step back and regarded me for a long moment. The frown on his face intensified. "The elders will not be happy if they find you on the ship."

"I'll be careful, I promise." I took his warning seriously. "If I get caught, it's on me. Besides, there's been so much talk that this virus is coming from the Vor'onins. If I could just find proof that it isn't true, then they couldn't blame you anymore, and then we could be together without hiding."

"I don't care what they say, I told you I will never leave you, not even the stars can tear us apart."

"I know, Jace, but if we can avoid fighting for the rest of our lives, then that's what I want."

He wasn't happy, but he didn't argue. It was the best I'd get from him so I went to my closet and pulled out a black, long-sleeved shirt and black workout pants to change into something less obvious.

Crossing the nearly abandoned city was eerie. It was like everyone had just… vanished. The only sign of life was the occasional light inside a few houses and the military tanks that roamed the streets. There weren't many, I was sure they didn't have the numbers they needed to police the entire country too closely.

The barricades were another story. Makeshift walls, that had to be about eight or nine feet high, had been put up in a hurry. Luckily, there were some gaps between them, but those were where the tanks were concentrated. No doubt it was probably intentional.

The smell of fire, mixed with a rancid note I couldn't identify, filled the air. I was afraid to ask what the source was, but morbid images of flames scouring high stacks of bodies sprang unbidden to mind. My stomach tightened, ready to revolt at the thought. I breathed through my mouth and tried to distract myself by thinking about Jace, and how he'd finally come for me.

It took us hours to get to the park, and by then I was exhausted. The only thing keeping me awake at that point was pure adrenaline.

We stood near the edge of the grass, hidden beneath the shadows of trees. I looked up. Without so many lights from the city, the stars sparkled across the night sky in a thick band. There were more than I'd ever seen before in my life.

"You know," I said as I started thinking back to my childhood, to when my brother and I would camp out in the backyard. Leaning against the trunk of the tree, hidden within its shadows, I intertwined my fingers through Jace's. "I used to look up at the stars and wonder if they ever looked back."

I tilted my head to the side to see him smiling warmly. I couldn't help myself, I reached out to pull him in for a quick kiss.

"Let's go," I said.

We jogged between the massive shadows the ships created between themselves, not stopping until we stood beneath a ship next to the one we wanted.

"Wait here. I have to open the ship and make sure no one is around to see you. I will return when it is safe. Stay in the shadows, Ray."

I warmed at the familiar use of my nickname. As far as I could recall, it was the first time he hadn't called me by my full name.

Jace stepped forward and held his hand out. A light shone from his palm. A symbol appeared, like a sideways, curved V with a dot in the center.

The ship came to life, responding to his command. Metal shifted fluidly without so much as a seam. I'd have sworn it was a living thing if I didn't know better. Steps formed from the entrance down to the grass. Nothing connected them, as they seemed to float in mid-air. Jace walked up and into the darkened maw of the vessel.

I waited for him to come back, but after twenty minutes, my confidence in his plan vanished. Fearing something had gone wrong, I chewed on my nails, biting them down to nubs. When Jace said he'd be back, I'd expected a few minutes—five tops.

Every rustle of wind through the trees had me jumping at shadows. The longer he was gone, the more I was worried that another crazy person would come after me.

And that's when I understood. Those men who'd run at me

had something seriously wrong with them, and it had happened twice in as many days in a city where I grew up never once having been chased or attacked.

I'd been so wrapped up in missing Jace the past few weeks, I never saw the connection until I was standing out in the cold, in the middle of the night, holding on to a leg of a space ship. I groaned and let my forehead hit against the pole. *Stupid. Stupid. Stupid.* I punctuated each word with a resounding smack.

"What are you doing?" Jace asked.

I stopped banging my head and looked up. "The guy who attacked me was sick with the virus," I said dumbly. When Jace didn't look surprised, I realized he'd already known. I pushed away from the metal leg. "I'm ready."

Jace paused a moment, studying me. "Stay behind me. There aren't many places I'll be able to hide you," he said.

"Why?"

"I don't like the idea of bringing you inside. It isn't safe, and I don't know what would happen if they found you."

"Jace, if they find me, I'll just explain why I made you bring me here. But I'll try not to get caught," I spoke with as much sweetness in my voice as I could, but when that didn't work, I dropped the smile and straightened. "Look, I don't want to believe… I *can't* believe that any of your people are responsible for this, but if they are, then my people have the right to know. Either way, we need to find proof. We all deserve to protect ourselves."

My stomach tied itself in knots. I felt bad implying the

Vor'onins might be responsible. But the fact of the matter was that either they'd released the virus, or the humans had.

It was sickening to think anyone could be capable of something so horrible, and on such a massive scale.

Jace cupped my face with one hand, and I leaned into it. I thought he was going to pull me in for a kiss, but he let his arm fall to the side. "Stay behind me."

I followed him up the steps. They wobbled under my feet as if adjusting to my weight. I almost squeaked in surprise as it shifted when I stepped off center. It took me twice as long for me to reach the landing to where Jace waited.

Inside, three tunnels led off of the bay. The main hall stretched out ahead of us, and two darker, narrower passages traced the edges of the ship, one on each side. Blue lights illuminated the space from the corners of the ceiling.

"It's best we stay out of the main areas," Jace said, turning to the right. "Char'ra is this way."

Walking quietly, I stayed as close to him as possible while trying to mimic the posture and grace. I'm sure I'd have looked insane if anyone had seen me, but thankfully, there wasn't a soul around.

There were several off shoots of narrow halls. This ship looked like a darker version of something you'd see in a sci-fi show, but the feel was the same, and I wondered if their bodies weren't the only things to have changed in stasis, or if their ships had changed to conform to our world as well.

The passage turned and we continued walking. At the end

were several doors, two of which were open. We stopped in front of the third.

Jace lifted his hand then glanced around.

"Come with me," he said, abruptly changing direction. He led me into one of the closed rooms. Metal crates were stacked up to a little over half my height. We wove between several towers until they hid us from view. "Wait here."

"Jace, no—"

"Someone might be in with Char'ra. I will come for you when it's clear," he promised.

Reluctantly, I did as he asked. Before ducking down, I looked around the room. The metal crates were everywhere. But on the far side, a room with glass walls. Inside several lab tables, and something that resembled a dentist's chair with a bright light overhead, sat. I didn't want to think about what it was for. Instead, I crouched low.

I heard the hydraulics of a door slide open and closed. Then silence filled the space, save for the soft hum of the engine.

After a while, my legs began to ache as I crouched behind the crates. I wanted to get up and stretch, or move around, but I didn't anticipate having to hide for much longer. Trying to distract myself, I looked at the metal boxes that surrounded me. Symbols were scrawled all over in silver lettering. They looked similar to the mark on Jace's palm.

I traced the lines of them with the pad of my finger trying to decipher their meaning, even knowing it would take years at best to read them. Something deep down told me that whatever the writing said, it was important.

Footsteps sounded along the corridor. *Jace was finally back!* Or that's what I'd hoped, until the sound of more than one set of boots echoing along the metal grate reached my ears.

My legs burned. I tried to adjust myself to a more comfortable position, but my cover was too low and I didn't want to call attention to myself in case it wasn't Jace. Though, I prayed he'd just brought Char'ra with him.

I strained to listen. Two male voices spoke low, growing louder as they drew closer.

"Doctor Lar'ruk, this is unacceptable, too many Vor'onins are vanishing. You've had a month to find a cure for this," someone said harshly. I knew his voice, but in that moment, I couldn't place where I'd heard it before.

Cure? I thought. It was all I could do to keep from hyperventilating. I'd come here in the hopes of finding proof that Vor'onins were innocent, and the first thing I'd come across sounded damning.

"Yes, Captain Thral'el," the doctor said in a nasally voice. "I have been doing my best, but I need more humans to test this on, or it will take years—"

"Our people do not have that kind of time!" Thral'el cut him off. "I expect results now. I don't care what you have to do."

I felt faint at the unspoken insinuations. *No, no, no, no, no!*

"I have found the cause…" the doctor started.

"Well, what is it?" Thral'el demanded.

"There has been a biochemical contamination. It seems

as though when certain Vor'onins come in contact with some humans, there is a biological response that creates an unwelcome outcome. I must study it more to understand the full implications." The doctor's voice grew higher in his excitement, getting faster with every word. "Our biology has become closer to theirs than was ever intended."

"How is that possible? We may look like them, but our DNA is vastly different."

"Several of the fleet across the globe malfunctioned during stasis, I suspect the ships were damaged during entry through the harsh atmosphere," the doctor's fervor had faded and his speech became halting. He cleared his throat. "If I could find what it was in their biology that causes this change in ours then I could use it to increase the effectiveness of the serum."

I bit down hard on my bottom lip and tried to keep my breathing slow. My legs were screaming in pain from crouching for too long. Red, hot pins and needles raced up my legs by the thousands. I was beginning to debate on which would be worse: staying like this or getting caught. And getting caught was looking really tempting with each passing second. My forehead started to break out in a sweat.

More footsteps on metal approached. *Why do they all want to congregate where I am?* I groaned inwardly.

"Jace'el, General Rath'ka, what a pleasant surprise it is, seeing you here," Thral'el said, though nothing in his tone indicated that he was pleased.

A deep, unfamiliar voice answered, "I found Jace'el entering as I left Char'ra's quarters."

There was a brief silence before anyone spoke. I could feel the tension increasing between them from my hiding spot.

"What do you need to speak to Char'ra about so late after sundown?" Thral'el asked pointedly.

"I came to see if she had any signs of finding my genetic match yet," Jace said.

I almost forgot my pain in that moment as my heart sank hearing his words. Had I imagined our connection, or was it a fabrication to cover for him seeking help?

"You've always resisted finding your match in the past. What has you so interested in finding your match all of a sudden? I can't imagine your time in restoration had been that effective."

Restoration? Was he injured after fighting with Josh? I wondered. *Or was restoration code for something worse?* I couldn't tell if Thral'el was suspicious, or pleased. Perhaps it was a little bit of both.

"If I am to take your place someday, then I must do what is required of me," Jace said firmly, with no emotion.

Needing to readjust some of my weight off my legs, I used the moment as an excuse to peer through a thin opening between a few crates. As I shifted, the toe of my shoe caught on the textured floor, making the tiniest ping. My ears burned from the noise.

Crap.

"Come with me," Thral'el said. "We will discuss this in private."

I listened to the sound of boots leaving and tried to count the number of pairs, but their different gaits threw me off. It was more than two, but it was impossible to tell if all of them had left or not.

I waited for another minute as they faded to nothing, and another moment after that before sucking in a sharp breath through my teeth, hissing.

One set of footsteps moved across the room. I had my answer. Blood drained from my face and my body went numb. I'd hoped they'd all left together, and I'd let my discomfort make me careless. It was impossible to tell what direction the last set of boots had headed. There was the smallest chance whoever it was hadn't heard me.

I clasped my hands over my mouth, trying to muffle the sound of my breathing. My eyes squeezed shut, and I pulled myself into a tight ball, willing whoever was there would pass by without noticing me.

Chapter Thirteen

Trial

A hand gripped my ponytail and jerked me up. Fire erupted along my scalp, forcing a cry from between my lips as it felt like every strand of my hair was being ripped from my head. The painful relief of my legs finally straightening only added to my discomfort as the blood flowed through them again.

When I opened my eyes, I stared into a man's face, one that would stay with me for the rest of my life. Teeth bared, narrowed ruby irises, and a scar ran down over his eye, cutting out a chunk of his eyebrow. He could have been handsome once, but in that moment, he terrified me.

He brought me close to his face and inhaled deeply. I cringed and tried to pull back, but his hold was too strong.

"Human…"

He was clearly not the nasally doctor, Lar'ruk. His voice was of the man who had come in with Jace... I struggled to remember. *Rath'ka?*

"Let me go, Rath'ka." I guessed, speaking through clenched teeth and hoping I'd gotten his name right. "Take me to Jace'el."

My hair slipped through his hand as he loosened his grip at Jace's name. Unprepared to support myself, I fell to the floor. I knew I'd remembered his name right when he didn't correct me, and even though I'd crashed onto the metal floor, I was freed from his clutches.

Rath'ka's hand wrapped around my upper arm and pulled me back to my feet. "I don't know what game you're playing at, but it won't work. If it were up to me, I would take care of you now."

I swallowed hard. I didn't know what he meant by "taking care" of me, but I didn't want to find out.

Swinging my legs, I landed a kick somewhere on his body. I used the momentum to bring my knee up hard into his abdomen. Immediately, a jolt swept through me, rendering my muscles useless. My limbs felt heavy, as if they had become stone, causing me to collapse on the floor, unable to move. It wore off quickly, but it weakened my will to fight.

Rath'ka dragged me out of the storage area and down the hall. My body could hardly manage to keep up and I struggled to stay on my feet.

The lights were brighter now as we moved back through the corridor the way I'd come with Jace. We reached the landing. He paused, and I'd dared to hope he'd just throw me out like a stray cat. But was disappointed when he moved to the wall, slamming his hand against it.

By the time we turned to face the main hall, there'd been enough of a commotion that several Others stood around, looking at me with something akin to fear in their eyes. I felt like a monster, barely contained by the rough General.

As I looked at them staring and whispering, I realized this was probably how Jace and the other Vor'onins felt when they came to our school. While I hadn't openly gawked at them, plenty had. The truth of it was, if I hadn't known Jace, I probably would have been one of them.

"Call the Council of Elders to convene," Rath'ka said as we passed a woman standing on the edge of the bay.

Before I could process his words, he dragged me down the main hall. Doors continued to open with curious faces peeking out. I struggled, trying to get him to loosen his grip, but he only tightened his hold.

"You're hurting me." I gritted my teeth against the pain. I could see the edges of my skin around his hand already changing to a bluish hue.

I stopped struggling when I realized we were in a poorly lit part of the ship. Boxes were pushed carelessly against the wall, their lids askew. A thick layer of grime coated the walls.

"Where are we? Let me go." I clawed at his hand to no avail. I was about as effective as a fly. My efforts only succeeded in making my arm burn as his hand chaffed my skin raw. I didn't like where he was taking me.

I hadn't expected this level of anger or aggression if I was caught. Jace had been right, but I'd been too stubborn to listen when he said he didn't want to bring me here.

A stale, rancid odor hit me as Rath'ka opened one of the many doors lining the walls. My eyes watered and I gagged, unprepared for the assault on my senses. I squinted into the room, but it was pitch black. The weak lighting of the hallway didn't reach inside. My imagination went wild at what awaited within the dark confines.

Rath'ka swung me forward by my arm. I tripped as my body lurched.

I hit the ground hard, my face coming in contact with the slick floor. I pushed myself up and looked over my shoulder just as the door slammed shut.

Groaning, I lifted my arm and tried to wipe the slime of the floor from my face, but I only ended up smearing it. I crawled, reaching out blindly until I reached a wall and leaned my back against it. The stench of the room became more intense after the door had shut. I pulled my knees up, hugging them to my chest, and rocked. It was all I could do to keep the tears from falling.

Jace would find me. He would get me out. I chanted those words to myself over and over until I lost track of time.

Click.

My head snapped up at the sound. Shivering in the sudden cold, I blinked into the dark, trying to make out anything that might be in the room with me. My body ached and there was a crick in my neck. I lifted a hand to massage the stiffness out. The chill of my hand surprised me. I must have fallen asleep.

A large figure stood in the door's opening. I quickly pushed myself up using the wall for support. I held my breath and hoped it wasn't Rath'ka. Every ounce of my body hurt. I couldn't take any more punishment. So I clung to the wall, not caring about the layer of film that covered it.

A female with blonde short cropped hair walked into the room, close enough for me to make out some of her facial features, and I breathed a sigh of relief that it was someone besides my least favorite General.

I took a step to the side to create more space between us as she stepped closer to me. She moved forward, unrelenting. Her hand reached out, and I turned my sore arm away so she'd grab the other. She grunted, annoyed, so I offered my other arm, too tired to put up another fight.

Pulling out a device that was a terrifying cross between a needle and a gun, she pressed it against the bruise on my arm.

"What are you doing?" I asked, wincing at the pressure on my tender skin. Ignoring me, she pulled the trigger. It hissed as it injected something into me, but rather than being drugged unconscious, the pain faded immediately, though the mark remained.

The woman put her needle-gun away and guided me from the cell. The light in the hall that had seemed so weak was almost blinding now as my eyes struggled to adjust.

My aching legs struggled to keep up with her long strides.

The ship felt so much bigger on the inside, but it was probably just my exhaustion catching up with me. I had no idea how much time had passed. It had been late when I left my house, but it had to be near morning by now. Soon, my family would be waking up and someone would realize I was gone.

Minutes later, I was dragged into a room, twice as wide as it was deep. In the center, there was a tall podium on a raised dais, with long benches on either side stretching out, and placed only slightly lower. Thral'el sat in the highest seat, with three others to his left and four to the right.

Spotlights lit them up, making the rest of the room feel infinite. Jace'el stood in front of his father's podium, his gaze to the floor.

The whole thing was surreal, like a trial from a nightmare. The weight of stares hefted upon me, from everyone in the room, was overwhelming. So many Others filled the room and I the only human. The sheer amount of bodies that filled the room made the temperature far warmer than the rest of the ship. I was willing to bet there were more here just to gawk at the human being subjected to this humiliation. I wondered if any of them had ever received this punishment, or if it was reserved for those unwelcome to their ships.

"We have gathered the high Council of Elders to judge and sentence this human." Thral'el started talking, but the second he uttered the word—*sentence*—my mind blanked.

The edges of my vision went dark and foggy, making focusing impossible. I heard words in my language, but struggled to understand the simplest meaning of anything said. The men and women on their high podiums spoke in hushed words.

I let my gaze wander until it finally rested on Jace, his face drawn. We were separated by such a short distance, only a few inches, but it might as well have been miles.

He looked as helpless as I felt. Jace looked up, and his face contorted as his eyes landed on my injured arm. I tried to turn it away. The last thing we needed was for him to react. The guard that gripped my arm tugged on me until I straightened my back and faced forward.

The sound of a pounding gavel made me jump, snapping me back to reality.

Jace looked ready to lunge over the waist high partition separating us. I opened my mouth to speak, but thought better of it. I shook my head and could only hope he understood.

The rustling and murmurs that had filled the room just seconds earlier went quiet. I looked around the room. Half of their attention was on me... the other half, on Jace. They had noticed something between us. I swallowed hard.

Thral'el glared down at me from his podium. He stood and leaned over the edge. His elongated shadow stretched out, eclipsing Jace and hovering over me like a demon ready to strike.

"You have been sentenced to twenty cycles in restoration."

Restoration... apparently my initial thoughts on what it meant were wrong. I had assumed it was something regarding healing, but other than a painful bruise, I wasn't injured. I hoped it wasn't a brainwashing system. I glanced at Jace from the corner of my eye. When we were apart, he'd gone through the same thing, though he never mentioned cycles.

"What's restoration?" I hated that my voice had a tremor in it.

"Silence," a man with silver hair and eyes boomed from the far right of the council. He had the perfect posture and confidence common in every Vor'onin I've seen, but his features were slightly aged.

"No!" Jace shouted, bringing my attention to him once more. His eyes hardened.

"You will be dealt with next, until then, you will be silent," Thral'el said.

"You can't do that," I protested, earning a room full of glares. "I didn't even get a chance to defend myself! I was just—"

"Whoever enters our ships is subject to Vor'onin law. You have been proven guilty of violating the non-entry treaty."

Off to the side, Jace's eyes were downcast. I didn't blame him for not fighting harder for me. It wouldn't have made a difference in the end. If anything it would have brought a worse fate, at least for him, if not for the both of us. We were helpless against the Vor'onins and against the world.

Opinions had formed, judgements made, and we had been found guilty of a crime I still didn't grasp. Jace would be punished alongside me, but the unknown of what our future held scared me.

On the way back toward the cell, I went willingly. I didn't have any fight left to give. Inside this ship, day and night were lost. I don't know how long I'd been there, but I did know enough time had passed that my family would know I was missing.

A pang in my heart made guilt spring up. I didn't even leave a note. For all they knew, I was gone and either the virus, or someone affected by it, had gotten to me.

They might never know the truth.

The ruby-eyed guard who led me away from the masses was quiet and looked less than pleased, but I was thankful she was much gentler than Rath'ka had been. I studied her as we walked. Though, she bared a resemblance to the man I'd grown to hate during my first trip down this hall, that just looking at her made my stomach turned leaden. With her softened features, and slightly slender, yet muscular build, I imagined this younger woman was what Rath'ka would have been as a female.

We reached my open cell and the guard let go. I walked inside on my own. It was a small thing, but I wanted to turn and thank her, but I resisted the urge. It was just my tired, aching body that was thankful. She might have been kinder, but she was still helping them keep me prisoner to punish me unjustly.

The door slammed shut. I walked with outstretched arms, feeling for the wall. The cold metal was the only source of comfort in this hell, and it was lacking in every way. Leaning against it, I slid down to the floor and wrapped my arms around my legs as the lock slid into place.

Exhaustion took over. My body shuttered. I was tired of fighting. This had turned out worse than I'd ever thought possible. Heat prickled my eyes and thick tears overflowed, burning streaks as they slid down my face. Sobs rose up my chest and caught in my throat.

I didn't understand what had happened during my sham of a trial. I didn't know what was going to happen to me. Self-pity washed over me like a wave of icy water.

Distant clanking came from outside my cell for a brief moment then left me in silence.

My sobs caught in my throat, and I tilted my ear in the direction of the sound, straining to hear more.

CHAPTER FOURTEEN

Test

I wiped my face with the heel of my hands and squinted into the dark. Scratching against metal sent a chill down my spine. I really hoped it wasn't rats, or worse, alien flesh eating rats.

No, stop it. You're just freaking yourself out. I chided silently.

A small square in the door opened and let the light from the hallway inside. I stood stiffly and walked carefully toward it.

"Raylinn?" Jace's voice whispered.

"Jace!" I ran and pressed myself to the cold, metal door. What I would have given to be able to have him hold me in that moment…

His fingers curled around the edge of the metal. I reached up and placed mine over his. The simple touch was enough for now. My eyes closed, and I rested my head on the metal separating us.

"Raylinn, are you hurt?" he asked after a while.

I thought about it. Cold, miserable, hungry, aching, exhausted? Yes, I was all of those things, but not hurt.

"No," I said truthfully, and Jace's fingers flexed beneath mine.

"Your arm," he said.

"It's fine." I said. "That one guard gave me a shot of something. It doesn't hurt anymore. I promise. It's just a bruise."

"I'll get you out of here as soon as I can," Jace said quietly.

"No!" I spoke louder than I'd meant too. "No, I don't want you to get in any more trouble because of me."

A rueful chuckle came through to my side. "Why can't you seem to remember what I told you? I will never let anyone keep us apart."

The corners of my mouth lifted despite the situation. "Whatever you do, please don't take unnecessary chances."

"I left that possibility behind the moment I followed you into that garden."

My heart hammered in my chest. So much had happened since that night; it felt like it had been a lifetime ago. I had no idea what would happen to me, but I wouldn't change a moment of my life since the ball to prevent it.

"What's going to happen?" I wasn't sure I wanted to know,

but hiding from it wouldn't save me.

"You will be in restoration for twenty cycles."

"I don't understand that." I shook my head even though I knew he couldn't see.

"Restoration is for you to stay in your cell. You will occasionally be brought out and volunteered for what the doctor needs you for."

"I won't let them use me as a lab rat. I have rights!"

"Not here," Jace said sadly.

"How long is a cycle?"

"A cycle is a year…" he said.

"Twenty years?" My hand dropped limply to my side. "No, they can't do that. My family, my government wouldn't—" I stopped. No one knew where I was. They wouldn't fight for me if they thought I was dead. And even if my family knew everything, I doubted the government would fight for a high school senior. No one would risk everything for someone who didn't even matter.

"You will never serve your sentence."

"Right, because I'll probably die in one of the good doctor's experiments," I spat out, slamming a fist against the door.

"I will get you out. I promise. I didn't bring you here to suffer like this. Wait for me, I'll be back soon."

Jace let his hand fall from the opening, then closed it. I listened to his footsteps fade as he walked away. I didn't know how he'd get me out, but I believed him.

Letting myself slump against the wall, I huddled in the corner and let myself drift into a restless sleep.

I woke with a start. Loud banging on the door made my head protest.

A slot in the door on the bottom opened and a bowl slid through. I reached forward and picked it up. In the dim light, I could see it was some kind of slop with the consistency of tapioca and the smell was something akin to warm milk. It didn't look appetizing in the least, but I was starving.

I stirred it then scooped up some of the gruel with the weirdly flat spoon before taking a bite. It was nearly flavorless and the texture was horrible. It was a mixture of chunks within a watery base with bits of squishy lumps and what I thought was, hopefully, half-cooked rice. I struggled to get it down. Closing my eyes, I lifted the dish to my lips and shoveled it into my mouth, trying to avoid breathing in the sour smell.

When I finished, I slid it back through the opening. A hand lifted the tray and closed the slot, leaving me in the pitch black once more.

Minute by minute, hour by hour, I could feel the eternal darkness breaking me. I began to wish for the experiments that I would suffer through for the next twenty years... or the death that would come from them. Anything to see the light again.

Time passed agonizingly slow. I waited, expecting Jace to return at any time. Minutes turned to hours and hours turned to days until I could no longer tell the difference between them. I must have paced my cell a dozen times. It was just as I had suspected—the only thing in this room was me.

At that point, it was obvious the hole I'd been thrown in was intentionally kept filthy, considering the rest of the ship was immaculate. A form of trying to break me psychologically. I hated to admit it, but it was beginning to work.

I managed to find a spot on the floor that was considerably less slimy than the rest of the room. I curled up, letting myself drift off to sleep.

I slept a lot. It was terrible quality sleep, which did little to refresh me. After a while, it was more out of boredom than being tired. There was only so much I could do within the empty room to pass time.

There didn't seem to be much of a schedule, it seemed I was just fed when they remembered I existed.

Maybe I wouldn't die a lab rat after all, but die of exhaustion and starvation instead.

It might have been days or weeks. Jace hadn't been by to see me since he promised to get me out, and I was beginning to give up all hope. The silence of my prison became a weight barring down, closing in to suffocate me, inch by inch, broken up only by the occasional hum of the ship.

At some point, the slot in the top opened. I jostled awake and scrambled to stand, falling against the door in relief.

"Jace!" I said.

"No, my little human," a nasally voice corrected.

I drew back as though he'd struck through the door.

"Wh-what do you want?" My throat burned, too dry from lack of water.

"It is time to begin," he said.

There was the click of the lock disengaging. The door swung open to reveal a skinny man who would have been attractive on some level had his presence not meant I'd be used as a guinea pig. I pressed a palm to my head. I was suddenly feeling confused. I stumbled.

The doctor reached out and gripped my arm, steadying me. I looked up into his face. My vision wavered, as if seeing two different versions of him. One that would have been overlooked in a crowd, and the other intense with a stare that could look into my soul.

"I am Doctor Lar'ruk," he said, leading me down the hall. His hand on my arm was light and more of a precaution in case I fell. There was nothing to keep me from running, yet I couldn't bring myself to try to get away.

"Where are we going?" I slurred.

Alarms went off in my head. My mind was screaming at me to run, to escape, that this man was dangerous, but my body followed every command he gave me, spoken, or with just the slightest pressure of his hand.

We reached a door and I paused as Doctor Lar'ruk opened it.

I glanced around, confused.

"How did we get here?" I asked.

"All in good time," he said, ushering me through.

The door closed behind us. We were in the storage room where I'd been caught, but we passed the countless crates and entered the lab enclosed by glass walls.

He led me inside and instantly, the glass became opaque. I licked my cracked lips trying to moisten them. I stood unable to do anything but glance around, no longer in control of my own body. Most of the tools and things in the room were unfamiliar to me, and in my hazy state, I couldn't even begin to identify or guess what they were for.

Lar'ruk fussed with several pieces of equipment, turning them on before walking to a cupboard I hadn't noticed, which had blended in with the wall.

He walked back to where I stood and handed me bundle of cloth. I looked at it, uncomprehending.

"Change into those," he commanded in a gentle voice that didn't seem to fit the situation.

Beyond my control, I watched in horror as my arms set the change of clothes down on the counter. My hands reaching for the hem of my shirt, lifting it over my head. I was a prisoner in my own body, and the man before me had utter control over every movement.

I wanted to vomit.

He stood in front of me, arms crossed as he considered me with cold, scientific scrutiny. I stood, completely naked for a painfully long moment before my hands reached for the clothes.

"Wait," he said.

My body obeyed. Tears filled my eyes, stinging before they fell down my cheeks.

The doctor moved to walk away then paused after a few steps to motion with a hand, "Follow me."

My feet took one step after another. I tried to resist, but all my effort didn't even cause me to hesitate. He led me to a small room with solid walls. My body walked into the corner and faced him, waiting on his next command.

"You are filthy." He reached past me.

My heart pounded in my chest. I wanted to cry out and push him away, but my body still refused to do anything. He pressed something on the wall, starting a stream of water.

"Wash." And with that, he turned away.

I let out a long, slow, relieved breath as my body washed itself. The water was lukewarm at best and lacked decent pressure, but after so long in the dank cell, it felt heavenly. I scrubbed the layers of grime off my skin until it was red.

My ribs protruded more than I remembered. I ran my fingers along the ridges. I'd lost a lot of weight. It was safe to say I'd been here for at least a few weeks. The urge to curl up on the floor and cry overwhelmed me. This place would kill me long before my sentence was up.

Why hadn't Jace helped me yet?

Just as I'd finished rinsing, the water abruptly shut off. I spun. Doctor Lar'ruk was standing behind me.

With a jerk of his chin, I walked toward him and took the offered towel from his hand.

After I dried, I walked back to the front. I hated feeling so powerless. Finally, I was slipping into the clothes he'd given me earlier. The clothes looked like a cross between white scrubs and a hospital gown. I faced the doctor and waited.

He regarded me with clinical scrutiny.

"What have you done to me?" I choked out. "How are you controlling me?"

"You have undergone the first test." He ignored my question and moved around the room. He picked up a tablet, using a stylus to write something down.

"What kind of test?"

"Control."

I gritted my teeth. My fists clenched at my sides as he continued to write, ignoring the fact that I clearly wanted a better answer.

Finally, he set his tablet down and gestured to the dentist-style chair. "Sit."

My eyes narrowed at the command even as my body obeyed.

The chair tilted back, and a large circular light overhead blinded me. I turned my head to the side. The doctor hovered around me, attaching wireless nodes to specific places on my head and torso.

Needles pierced my arms at the elbows, my hands, and just when I'd thought he was finished, one pierced the center of my chest. Other than the tremble that swept my body as I gasped, I lay still. My muscles refused to move, even as my mind screamed to rip away everything he'd attached to me and run.

The doctor hovered above me. "When I came to collect you from your cell, you called me Jace—did you mean Jace'el?"

I nodded.

"Why would you think Jace'el would come to your cell? He is not a guard," he said. The expression on his face was amused rather than confused at my over familiarity with Jace.

I bit the inside of my cheek and tried to stay quiet, but I was still under his command. "I-I thought he would rescue me."

"He has been under surveillance these past weeks."

At least there had been a reason. It was a small comfort that he hadn't abandoned me.

Doctor Lar'ruk leaned in, his face so close we were almost touching. My breath caught.

"I know what has happened between you. I suspect his father knows only part of it. If he knew everything, your punishment would have been far worse." He spoke slowly, his voice barely above a whisper. "Jace'el is important to us."

I swallowed hard. "How do you—"

"I used pheromones to control you, but they were only effective to getting you to obey me. That would not have been the case if you had never met Jace'el."

"Will you tell Thral'el?"

"No," he said, leaning back in his chair.

Hope sprang in my chest.

"Why not?" I asked. *He knew,* and if he were willing to keep this information to himself, maybe he would help me.

"Relax," he said before I could beg. "We are just checking your overall health to see how you will handle future sessions."

My heart sank. He still planned on using me as a test subject against my will. I stopped fighting and gave in. I could feel his will over me ebb and flow as if he were testing to see what I would do.

But I didn't care anymore. I was stuck here, doomed to be experimented on, most likely until I died. And Jace would be helpless to rescue me.

By the time the doctor had finished his examination, his will over me was gone.

"You may sit up now," he said.

I did as he told. What difference would it have made if I'd forced him to make me move? If I had even thought of doing anything, he would only control me again.

I hung my head as we took the long walk back to my cell, my feet shuffled along the floor. Any hope I'd had before was crushed like glass over rocks.

All too soon, I found myself back in the black hole that was my new home, alone for hours on end—days. The doctor didn't return anytime soon, and neither did Jace. I tried to keep track of the meals they brought to me. I assumed it was once a day at most. Sadly, it was the only thing left in my life to look forward to.

Boredom got the best of me, and I made a point to do simple exercises to pass the time. Push-ups, lunges, crunches—nothing too strenuous. I wanted to regain some of my strength, not lose more weight.

I laid on my back, just having finished a round of crunches as sweat rolled down my temples, when the lightest scratching sound brought me to full alert. I sat up and strained to hear.

The upper slot in the door slid open.

"Raylinn?" Jace's voice asked from the other side. His voice was honey to my ears. I closed my eyes for a second and let the sound wrap itself around me.

I stood and ran to the door, reaching out the small opening with my fingers.

"Jace?" I asked hardly daring to believe.

CHAPTER FIFTEEN

Break

"Jace," I breathed his name. It felt strange to talk after not using my voice for so long.

I was either crazy, or he'd finally come for me!

"Raylinn, I want you to take this," he said. His hand slipped through the opening and offered me a small, glass object.

Pale bioluminescent light lit up my dingy cell. The small particles within danced, throwing specks of light against the walls like billions of swirling stars dancing in the night sky.

"What should I do with this?"

"Wait," Jace said. He had a habit of not explaining things to me. I wondered if it was a Vor'onin trait, as the doctor seemed to suffer from the same problem. Jace slipped a hand through to my side of the cell and cupped my face. I leaned into him and closed my eyes, missing the warm, familiar touch. It had been so long since I'd felt any touch at all. Loving, hateful, or scientific. The feel of his skin on mine made tears burn my eyes.

"You will come back for me this time?" I asked in a small voice filled with fear, worried it would be longer than the last time before I saw him again.

"I'm sorry about my long absence, but I will explain in time. For now, be ready."

Jace reluctantly pulled away, leaving me to feel colder than before. I listened to his footsteps as he walked away. When I couldn't hear anything but the quiet hum of the ship, I stepped back. Part of me tried to will Jace back to me. I was so tired of being alone.

After several moments, when he didn't return, I let the light of the small orb guide me to the spot against the wall I'd been at before he'd come.

I rubbed the ball between my palms, playing with the shadows it created between my fingers. Footsteps pulled me out of the peaceful trance I'd managed to lull myself into. I stayed seated and waited for my visitor to identify themselves.

The door opened and the thin doctor's silhouette framed the doorway.

Figures, I thought.

The doctor had this habit of coming to see me almost immediately after Jace. Almost as if he'd planned it. Tightening my fist around the tiny ball of light, I shoved it into my pocket as

I stood and made my way over to him. The more I complied, the less he did to control me.

Even if my actions were the same as if he were in control, at least I was making the conscious effort to do so rather than being forced. If that was the only battle I could win, then I would take it.

"It is time for your first test," he said as if we were headed out for a nice lunch.

"You time your visits," I said aloud, a statement more than a question. "You wait for something to happen before coming to get me."

I didn't have to say Jace's name. We both knew who I was talking about.

Doctor Lar'ruk cleared his throat. He brought his face close to mine as if he were about to impart a secret.

"Yes, I—" He stopped abruptly as the hum of the engines increased before fading, taking the light with it. I swung my hand, hitting him in the head with my glowing orb. Then Doctor Lar'ruk fell to the floor in a heap.

A dark shadow moved quickly. I pressed myself against the wall, barely stifling a scream.

"Ray," Jace's voice whispered through the dark.

Relief swept through me and I dropped my arm. He smiled through the dim light, and I fell into his arms for an all too brief embrace. Sooner than I wanted, Jace pulled away and dragged the doctor's limp body into my cell before closing the door.

"Come, we don't have much time."

Jace took my hand and led me through the halls. I hadn't even begun to memorize them, but they looked so different in the dark.

After making our way down several passages, I slowed. "Where is everyone?"

"It is the middle of a sleep cycle. Most won't realize what has happened until the sun rises, but there are guards in the halls."

I silenced any further questions I had.

The main hall was in sight and Jace upped the pace. We rounded the corner and he came to an abrupt halt. I bumped into him. He spun, grabbed me by the shoulders and pressed me into a dark cove. He pulled the door closed, leaving the smallest opening to look through.

I didn't need him to tell me to keep quiet. I trusted him to do what he needed to get me out safely. I clutched the blue orb tightly to my chest to keep the light hidden.

Someone with a heavy gait approached, then another lighter step sounded from the other direction, stopping in front of Jace. I strained to listen, but I couldn't make anything more out.

"There you are," Jace said, as if he'd expected that particular guard to show up.

"Jace'el, what are you doing out of your quarters?"

"I don't answer to you," he said indignantly. "I was up when the power went, but no one seems to be doing their job around here."

There was a long pause between them. I assumed the guard wanted to question Jace, but status prevented him from doing so. According to the doctor, Jace was important to them, but he never explained how.

A thought occurred to me as I stood in the dark corner. If Jace was so important, did they see my presence as a threat? What was I putting in jeopardy being with him? We had come to the ship to find answers. Answers that would have benefited everyone, but what if my presence only made things worse?

"Are you going to stand there all night, or are you going to figure out what happened and fix it? I doubt Thral'el would be pleased to see such lethargic behavior. Go, down that hall. I've already checked this one," he said. "Report back to me if you find the source of the power outage."

"Yes, Jace'el," the guard replied.

Boots stomped down the way we had come.

A moment later, Jace pushed open the door and slid inside with me. It was a tight fit and we were pressed against each other. Not that I minded.

"What are we doing?"

"We must be quick. If anyone sees you, they will sound an alarm. If we're caught, I won't be able to get you out again. Your punishment will be more severe if you are caught again. I need you to understand the risk."

I nodded. "If we get caught, then I doubt it would be much worse than what my life would have been. At least this way I have a chance."

"You can leave the light here. This last part is too open; it will call attention to us before we are ready."

I closed the door behind us. With my hand in his, he led me through the wide hall. I itched to run to the exit but forced myself to keep slow and quiet.

We were halfway to the door when the sound of boots pummeling against the metal floor grew louder as they approached. I squeezed Jace's hand, but he kept me at the same pace. The whole time my heart pounded mercilessly against my ribs. My breaths came in short bursts.

"Stop!" a voice boomed.

Jace didn't even look back. He pulled on my arm and ran. I struggled to keep pace with his long strides, taking twice the number of steps. The hum of engines restarted and the lights flickered back on.

We were exposed.

He picked up the pace and I stumbled. My hand was ripped from Jace's grasp as I hit the ground. He skidded to a stop and turned back for me. But the thunder of boots grew ever louder.

I pushed myself up and scrambled toward Jace, panting hard. I'd come too far to lie down and give up.

Forcing my body to keep stride, we managed to keep ahead of them. We slammed into the wall where we'd entered.

"Jace?" my voice trembled as I looked behind us.

He pressed his hand against the wall and the glow from the symbol on his hand grew brighter. A high-pitched squeal sounded. I snapped my eyes to his face. His mouth hung open in shock.

"I-I've been blocked from opening the ship."

We were seconds from being caught. I would die here and I'd never see Jace again. I felt my mind go blank. All I could see was the threat coming toward us. The threat that would mean I'd die without ever seeing the sun again.

I gritted my teeth and ran toward the closest guard. I would rather die now than slowly and painfully over years of experiments. The guard hesitated. His pace slowed. I hit him with the full force of my weight in the gut.

It wasn't much, but I pushed off the ground with all the strength of my legs. His hand lifted but I managed to avoid the shock I knew would be delivered if I let him touch me.

He hit the ground hard. His head smacked against the floor and he stilled.

Another body fell as I blinked down at the guard under me. I pulled back my arm and punched him in the jaw. I wanted to make sure he was out and not just faking. Part of me, maybe the bigger half, just wanted the satisfaction of hitting the man who was trying to prevent me from regaining my freedom.

Lifting myself up, I saw Jace. He'd taken care of the other guard. He dragged him in the direction of the door. I helped him lift the limp man.

Jace used the guard's palm to open the door then let him drop to the ground in a heap.

An opening in the side of the ship formed and the metal reshaped into steps. We waited anxiously, knowing more guards would be coming soon.

The steps were halfway formed when we started down them,

and before they fully created a path to the ground, we jumped.

I landed hard on the ground and rolled. Jace landed in a crouch and straightened immediately. He reached out and offered me a hand up.

We were out, but not safe. The adrenaline that had brought me this far was fading.

"Jace," I breathed. "I can't…"

He didn't take my protests, and pulled me after him. As much as I wanted to stop, as fierce as my lungs burned and muscles protested, I didn't fight him. We ran through the park and made our way toward the nearest barricade. We were so close and the Vor'onins wouldn't dare follow us past it.

Would they?

It seemed as though Jace had scouted the area and memorized the smallest opening, one hidden by overgrown bushes. He pushed them aside, and we passed through, letting the branches and leaves fall back into place.

I stopped running and bent over. I rested my hands on my knees to catch my breath. My sides hurt, and my legs threatened to collapse out from under me. I was thankful for the exercises I had done, but it hadn't been enough. Much of my muscle mass had shrunk during my time imprisoned and combined with the lack of sufficient calories, I was weak.

"Come, we can't rest yet."

I wanted to argue, but instead allowed him to lead the way. The streets were abandoned. Cars sat parked on the side of the road, covered in a thick layer of dust and pollen. But the further we ventured into the sectioned off area, the creepier it became. A few cars were stopped in the middle of the street as if people had vanished into thin air without warning.

We wove through several blocks, zigzagging as we went. Windows were broken and shops were emptied. I wrapped my arms around myself.

Buildings eventually made way to houses as we crossed several more barriers dividing the city. My legs shook with each step and it was all I could do to keep from falling on my face from exhaustion. I don't remember when we'd slowed from a run to a walk.

"Jace," I panted, "I need to stop. Please, I can't go any further."

He really looked at me then, as if he was only seeing the toll my time on the ship had on me for the first time. Jace pulled me to him and kissed the top of my head.

"Just a little further. There is a house we can stop at a few blocks from here."

I swallowed and fought back the tears, determined to stay strong if only for a few minutes longer.

It felt like hours later when we approached a pale yellow house with white trim and a red door. The doors and windows were closed and the lights off. But that was normal for this time of morning. A single car was parked in the driveway, just as dusty as the rest.

The sky was the sickly grey that comes just before the brilliant hues of dawn.

"Jace, this house doesn't look empty," I muttered.

He gave me a sympathetic look before speaking. "There are no humans left in this sector. They have all evacuated, or died from the virus. I've already scouted this area."

That explained our erratic path. We were avoiding bodies and tanks. I followed him to the back of the house. Glass from the shattered sliding door lay scattered on the back porch. Streaks of blood covered several shards. We stepped inside, the crunch of glass under my shoes filled the empty space.

The house looked as though people had been going about their everyday life before they'd left. There was no sign of struggle or anything… at least if you ignored the back door. I wondered what happened to cause them to break glass but leave everything else untouched. I hoped they'd evacuated rather than died of the virus.

I walked though, immediately heading for the pantry in the kitchen. I threw open the door, my hands shaking from hunger. A whimper escaped me at the sight of canned fruit. I grabbed several cans and set them on the table before raiding the kitchen until I found utensils.

Jace waited by my side as I ate three cans, only slowing down once I opened the fourth.

"Where did everyone go when they evacuated?" I asked between mouthfuls.

"The last time I checked, they were being pushed toward the outer sectors to the east. Those infected have been kept within the confines of the inner sectors. Once there are too many cases of the virus, they lock it down, and the healthy who are unlucky enough to still be there when that happens are stuck."

I swallowed the bite I'd been chewing and pushed it away, no longer hungry.

"My parents?" I asked.

"Their sector is safe for now." Jace placed a hand over mine. I still had a home to go back to.

I looked down at myself. "I'm going upstairs to look for a change of clothes and see if they have running water. I can't go home like this."

Jace pushed back his chair and followed me upstairs.

There were four bedrooms in total, and it was the last I found a closet with women's clothing. I picked out a pair of yoga pants and a thin shirt. They were a little big for me, but they were better than nothing.

I headed into the master suit bathroom, leaving Jace stretched out on the queen-sized bed.

The bathroom was the size of a small studio. A deep bath sat centered against the window, the toilet was around the corner to the left—*the room was big enough to have a corner.* The double sink was on the far right.

Behind the bath, the window stretched from floor to ceiling. It was tinted, but I walked over and closed the blinds anyway. The last thing I wanted to do was call attention to our presence here.

I tested the faucet, surprised to see that it worked. Setting the plug, I let the hot water run over my hand as I waited for it to fill.

I undressed, kicking my clothes into the corner, glad to be rid of them. I never wanted to see those prison clothes again.

I inched my way into the water and let the heat scald my skin, turning it red. I scrubbed and scrubbed, trying to wash off the layer of slime that had become a part of me over the last few weeks, trying to wash away everything I'd been through.

The water was darker by the time I finished. I let it drain then refilled it adding in some scented salts I'd found. Leaning back, I closed my eyes and let my sore muscles relax.

Chapter Sixteen

First of Many

"Raylinn."

I woke with a start. My knees buckled and I slipped down the slick porcelain. Water splashed my face and went up my nose. I coughed as I resurfaced. I wiped my face off as I sat up in the now cool water.

Jace stood above me, holding a towel.

Blinking up, I rubbed my bleary eyes. I went to speak, but whatever I was going to say turned into a yawn. He knelt down and pulled the plug. I took up the towel and wrapped it around my body. Jace offered me a hand as I stepped out. It probably saved me from landing on my face.

He wrapped his arms around me and kissed the top of my head. I snuggled into him, enjoying the warmth and safety.

With his help, I made my way into the bedroom and dressed. I ran my fingers through my hair trying to get some of the tangles out, but gave up after a minute.

I plopped down on the bed, my legs dangling off the edge. My eyes grew heavy, and I was tempted just to fall asleep like that. Jace pulled the covers back and somehow managed to drag my lower half up to crawl under the down-filled blankets.

He got into bed next to me and pulled me close. I rested my head on his chest and listened to his heart. It beat slowly on the right side of his chest.

"I don't know what I'm going to tell them," I murmured, letting the beat lull me.

"Tell who?" Jace asked.

"My family." I tilted my head back to meet his eyes. "I don't want to lie to them, but I can't tell them where I've been or what happened."

"Then tell them only what they need to know," Jace said. He lifted a hand and stroked my head.

Another yawn escaped and I snuggled deeper into Jace's side, falling asleep within seconds.

***

The sun was setting by the time I peeled my eyes open. My heart pounded. I frowned, unable to remember my dreams, or if I'd had any.

I wasn't sure why I was awake, but I knew something had

woken me. Grudgingly, I listened for a moment instead of falling back to sleep. All I heard was the hum of a silent house.

I shrugged it off, content to allow myself to sleep the rest of the day and through the night.

A clatter of pans echoed from downstairs. I shot up, clutching the blanket to my chest. I'd let myself get too comfortable.

Jace stirred beside me and sat up. "What's wrong?"

"I heard something," I whispered. My fingers wrapped around his arm.

We threw back the covers and grabbed our shoes, slipping them on before making our way to the doorway.

Jace looked back to me. I took a deep breath and nodded that I was ready. Together, we walked down the stairs as quietly as we could. Another rustle of pots scattering.

The noise came from the kitchen, but we looked around all the corners just in case there was someone hiding in wait. It was impossible to tell if the homeowner had returned, or if other survivors had the same idea as we had.

I wished I had a baseball bat, or golf club, anything to protect myself. But I didn't. I just clenched my fists. My body already tense, preparing to fight or run at any second.

Pressing our backs to the wall, we peered into the kitchen. The noise had stopped. I frowned up at Jace and stepped inside.

A man in a dirty suit snapped his head in my direction and ran at me in the time it took for me to blink. I barely had a chance to inhale as he reached me. My fist shot out and hit him square in the nose. I felt the crunch of brittle bone break beneath my fist.

He collapsed on the linoleum floor, groaning.

Jace and I didn't wait for him to get up. We took off at a run and didn't stop to breathe until we were several blocks away, in a park I'd never been to.

It was open and I hated feeling exposed. My gaze darted in all directions, making sure no one was coming at us. Jace's soft laughter broke my focus, and I turned to him.

"What's so funny?" I asked with a raised eyebrow.

"If I didn't know better, I'd say you were able to defend yourself the same way as a Vor'onin with how hard that man hit the ground."

"Yeah, well, he startled me," I mumbled. My face warmed. I'd never actually punched anyone before.

My hand throbbed from the impact. No one ever tells you that part. It always looks so easy and pain free. I could still move all my joints so I knew nothing was broken, but I was unprepared for how much it would hurt. Movies had really given me unrealistic expectations.

After I'd caught my breath, we continued on as we had yesterday. Even in the dark, we wove our way through the city, taking the alleys as often as we could to avoid any tanks or crazed people that might be around.

We neared my neighborhood around dusk. It was a long walk, but having to stay hidden made it even longer. I paused when I didn't hear Jace's constant footsteps behind me.

Glancing over my shoulder, I saw him standing in the middle of the road just staring into the distance.

"Jace?" I called. "What are you doing? Someone is going to see you."

I ran to his side and tugged on his arm.

"I have to see if he's all right."

"What? Wh—" I followed his gaze to a tall figure that could only belong to one of the Vor'onins.

"Something's wrong, I have to check on him."

"Jace, no, what if they are looking for me? I don't want to go back." My voice trembled. I let go of his arm. I didn't understand why he wanted to go near the ones responsible for my days or weeks of torture.

Jace ignored my protests and walked nearer. I hung back, not sure I'd be able to outrun one of them if they tried to come after me. This could be a trick meant to play on his instincts in an attempt to flush us out. He stopped a few yards away. Entirely too close for my comfort.

The alien turned toward Jace with jerky movements, stumbling after him. Even from this distance, I could tell something was wrong.

"Jace!" I clapped my hands over my mouth too late to stop the scream from ripping its way out of my throat.

Thankfully, he backed away in time.

He stayed out of reach and continued to talk while avoiding the other man's ungraceful attempts at grabbing him. When the other man collapsed and lay still, I ran to Jace's side.

I looked down. His skin had a sickly yellow tint. The hollow of his cheeks were unhealthy, as if he was wasting away faster than natural. His chest rose and fell in shuttering breaths.

"Do you know him?"

Jace shook his head.

"What's wrong with him?"

"It is an illness I'm not familiar with." Jace gripped his chin and looked at the Vor'onin, studying him.

I backed away slowly. The sick alien blinked up as if not quite understanding. His skin was pale and almost translucent with a yellowish tint. He coughed, his whole body violently shaken by the fit. A droplet of blood formed in the corner of his mouth and dribbled down his chin. His breathing became more uneven and shallow. Then stopped.

The blood drained from my face. We'd stood here and watched him die. *We let him die.* I felt so heartless, even though I knew there was nothing we could have done to prevent it. I could have provided comfort, held his hand. Something—*anything*.

I looked around, trying to remember where we were through my shock.

"We need to go." I pulled Jace's hand, backing away from the body. I could hear shouts in the background and the sound of unfamiliar heavy machinery. Reluctantly, he followed.

We passed through two more barricades before stopping again. People crying and orders being thrown around in the typical military tone could be heard in the distance. Judging by the previous barricades, my home was still two sectors away.

I looked Jace up and down. He could almost blend in, but not in his typical Vor'onin clothing. It stood out, even in the dark. I didn't want to take him into a crowd of people who might attack… or worse, *kill* him just for not being human. Though I hadn't really thought of him as an alien for a while. He was just Jace to me.

"I don't know how safe it will be for me to get through the next barricade."

He must have been thinking the same thing as me. He moved back almost as if he thought I could go on without him. I straightened my spine and rested my fists on my hips.

"We need to find you new clothes to wear." I looked around the neighborhood until I spotted a house with a sports car with flames on the side out front. That house would be our best bet. "Come on."

I didn't give him a chance to protest. I dragged him to the house, praying it was empty.

Out of habit, I knocked. No one answered after a few attempts so I tried the doorknob. It opened without resistance. Silently, Jace followed me through the house as I stuck my head into every room.

"What are we doing?" he asked.

"Finding you something to wear so you can blend in."

Finally, I found what I was looking for. A messy room with an unmade bed, clothes strewn about, and posters of bikini models and cars plastered along the wall. The air was stale, but I ignored it and rummaged through the closet.

I pulled out a large hoodie with some company's logo across the front with a pair of jeans I hoped would fit, and handed them to Jace. "Put these on."

The look on his face when he took the clothes would have been hilarious if it wasn't for the seriousness of the situation.

Jace changed as I rummaged through the room for one last item. I grabbed a pair of sunglasses off the stereo and turned back to him. The thickness of the hood was high enough to hide the three scar like marks on either side of his neck, and the jeans were a near perfect fit. Jace looked like every other high school guy.

"Here," I said, handing him the glasses. "Put them on before we cross the barrier. They'll hide your eyes."

He frowned but didn't argue.

Getting to the other side of the barricade was easier than I'd expected with the massive crowds. Men in uniforms were separating people without prejudice. Most complied with the orders given, but an occasional group of people would protest and fight, resulting in a blow to the head from the butt of a gun, or zapped with a taser. Dark personalities brought to the front and set free by the chaos.

Jace and I moved seamlessly through the crowd, heading in the direction of my house as best we could without drawing attention to ourselves. I clung to his hand as we wove our way through.

"You two, over here!" a man demanded as he stopped us with his palm up. He held his gun across his body, his trigger finger twitching to move into position at a moment's notice.

"Raylinn? Raylinn Marrow?" a man's voice asked.

I turned to the origin of the voice and saw a man I didn't recognize calling my name. His blond hair was greasy, as if he used too much product. He smiled at me with large, white teeth and blue eyes. Freckles dotted the bridge of his nose, giving him a boyish look that didn't quite fit with the wrinkles at the corners of his eyes.

I clutched tighter to Jace's hand, unsure how this strange man knew me.

"It's me, Fred McCloy. I work with your father," he explained as he approached.

"Oh, hi," I said awkwardly. "I didn't recognize you."

"It's been a while—" he started.

"Sir, you need to move back to your line," the soldier interrupted.

"She needs to come with me. I know her family," Fred said. My jaw dropped. I was about to argue when he grabbed my arm, pulling me away from Jace. "She's a minor. Her family lives this way, I'll make sure she gets home to them."

"Let me go," I said, trying to pull away.

Fred looked at me as if I was incapable of making a decision. Maybe that's how he saw me, but it didn't calm the anger rising up inside me.

"Do you have any idea how worried your family is? They've been calling everyone for weeks."

"I can make it home without you," I insisted. "Please let me go. I can't leave Jace—"

"Your boyfriend will be fine without you; he needs to make

his own way home. I'm taking you to your father, he'd kill me if he knew I found you and didn't take you home myself."

At that moment, I wasn't worried about this strange man's life. I was worried for Jace. The crowd pushed Jace deeper and deeper into the thick of it.

Somewhere, a man let out a savage cry as if he were dying. A horrible sound that silenced everyone.

"Runner!" a woman screamed. Her voice cracked and turned into a blood curdling noise of horror and pain.

I looked to the far side of the crowd. People were fleeing from a central point in the fray.

The shot of a gun rang out. Then several more.

It didn't take much to connect the dots. I'd been chased by many infected. They zeroed in on someone with a single purpose in mind—to attack mindlessly.

The first I'd seen was the man when I bordered the light rail; he'd locked on me, his fingers clawed against the door until they bled, trying to get through.

Time slowed and sped up simultaneously. People began shoving everyone else around them, trying to get away. Military personnel tried their hardest to keep everyone in order, with little luck.

"Jace!" I called desperately, searching for his face and hoping he'd manage to make his way to me. I stood on my toes trying to see above the sea of heads.

"Raylinn! Ray!" Jace called out. I turned toward his voice and he was already behind a barrier.

The wrong barrier. My heart sank. *No!* I didn't want to have him taken from me again.

Mr. McCloy pulled me along, ignoring my protests. I knew his heart was in the right place, but I was sick of being dragged against my will by everyone who thought they knew better than me, thought they had a right to decide my fate for me. I didn't fight. I didn't want to be mistaken for a *runner.*

"Jace!" I cried. My hand reached toward him as if I could cross the distance by sheer will.

He tried to take a step toward me, but soldiers pushed him back in the direction of yet another barricade.

"Find me!" I mouthed, my hand still hopelessly reaching for him.

Jace nodded and then let the crowd swallow him.

CHAPTER SEVENTEEN

Sound of Melancholy

I let out a frustrated groan.

"I don't need your help," I snapped, jerking my arm from Fred's grasp.

"Everyone needs someone's help. It isn't an insult to you, so don't take it personally," he said, guiding me, with barely restrained force, along the line toward a sector closer to my home.

"Yeah, well you separated me from the one person who was helping me."

"Stop concerning yourself with a high school crush. You can find him again once things get back to normal." His growing condescension only added fuel to my anger.

The soldiers guided us through an opening in a high fence, which had barbed wire rolled along the top.

"This isn't about a crush," I argued, unable to let it go. "He has nowhere else to go, and now you made me abandon him after everything he's done."

Mr. McCloy didn't respond for a long time.

A line of soldiers held the crowd at bay like a herd of sheep. One stepped forward and said in a booming voice, "Go, if you have a place to stay on this side of the barricade, I suggest you get there in the next hour or two. Anyone caught out after dark will be arrested or shot."

People pushed faster as fear spurred them on. The government had gone to extremes. Threatening to kill innocent people for being out at night. It was too much, but their demeanor made it clear it wasn't just a threat. They meant every word.

"I'm sorry I separated you two, but you have to understand how worried your family is."

We walked side by side, but his hand still held my arm. It gave me flashbacks of Rath'ka, if only less violent.

My stomach felt uneasy. There was no way for me to find Jace now. I could only hope he'd be able to find me later.

There were two more barricades to pass before we reached my neighborhood. We rounded the corner as the sun disappeared over the horizon. As much as I wanted to run and leave this man behind, I kept my pace steady. I still wasn't sure what to say to my parents. I realized then that my father's friend hadn't even asked me where I'd been for weeks—not that I'd wanted him to, but it struck me as a little strange. Perhaps he didn't care. For all I knew, he was doing this "good deed" to gain some kind of favor from my father. After all, I would have seen a lot more of him if he'd lived near us.

I opened the door to my house and the familiar smell of home greeted me. I never thought I'd see home again. Relief came over me and instantly felt how drained I was.

Toby looked away from the TV and stared at me for a few seconds before understanding hit him.

"Ray!" he yelled. Toby jumped up from the couch and ran to me. He hugged me just as my parents burst through the kitchen door, stopping when they saw me. It was awkward; we were never the type of siblings who hugged.

"Oh my God, Ray!" Mom cried, rushing to wrap her arms around Toby and me. My dad joined a second later.

"Where have you been?" Dad asked once everyone had let go and I was able to breathe again.

"I found her a few sectors away," Mr. McCloy volunteered.

I'd forgotten about him. The man did not know when he was unwelcome.

"Fred?" Dad met him at the door and clapped him on the back. "Thank you for bringing her home to us."

"Oh, honey," my mom turned away from the men and spoke directly to me. "You look so skinny!"

"It's okay. There was just a shortage of food." It wasn't

exactly a lie. I didn't have access to much food where I'd been.

Mom led me to the kitchen and immediately started rummaging for food. Toby walked in a second later and sat next to me at the table. The frown, the hug… he'd been worried.

"Where have you been, Ray?" he asked.

I'd hoped for more time before the questions started, but it was understandable that they were desperate to know.

"I was out for a run. I didn't think I'd get another one for anytime soon, so I wanted to take advantage of it while I could. I guess I went too far and ended up stuck behind one of the first barricades. They held me in quarantine for a few weeks to make sure I wasn't infected," I explained, making sure to leave out who *they* were. It was the truth. A twisted, misleading version, but far better than admitting I was held prisoner and about to be turned into a lab rat for the Vor'onins.

The men joined us just as Mom set a sandwich in front of me.

"I'm sorry I don't have anything better, we're running low on food. We haven't been able to make it to the store this entire time," Mom explained.

"Fred will be staying with us. The sector his house was in has been evacuated." Dad looked between Toby and me. "You two will share a room, and Fred will take Ray's room."

My jaw dropped. This guy didn't even seem phased by taking over my space. He'd done nothing but make a crappy situation worse. He just took what he wanted, regardless of the effect he had on others' lives.

"I'm not sharing a room with her." Toby spoke up before I had a chance. "Besides, Ray's been gone for weeks dealing with who knows what. I'll take the couch, he can have my room."

"Fine, Fred will take Toby's room."

I'd never been so happy to have my brother on my side as I was in that minute. I mouthed a silent *thank you* to him, then went back to finishing the last bites of food. Toby stood and squeezed my shoulder with one hand before heading upstairs.

Dad and his friend stood around while my mother continued to flit around the kitchen, trying to take care of everyone.

I popped the last bite in my mouth and pushed back my chair. I'd missed my family, but I needed a sanctuary where I could retreat into and give my mind a break from the insanity that had turned the world upside down. I needed a moment to pretend life was exactly the way I remembered it.

"I'm going upstairs to shower and sleep. It's been a long day," I announced. I started up the stairs when the blare of the local news station's bulletin stopped me in my tracks. A somber reporter frowned as she spoke.

In the wake of the worldwide pandemic, the citywide lockdown has widened its parameters. Similar lockdowns have been reported across the globe as more and more cases of the Nightshade virus continue to spread. Little is known on how it's transmitted. Scientists have speculated that some of the population may have a natural immunity to the virus, but might be unsuspecting carriers. The CDC urges everyone to stay inside and report cases of contamination to authorities immediately. President Birchfield will be meeting with his cabinet later today to sign the CEA, the Contamination Epidemic Act, into law, making it mandatory to report any and all suspected cases.

This just in—the sectors between south east Morrison Street and the Burnside Bridge will be evacuated within two days. Each person is allowed one bag and must be able to carry it themselves due to the division of sectors. Any illnesses upon reaching the barricades must be reported.

Images of my neighborhood flashed across the screen. The news anchor was talking about our sector. I'd only just managed to make my way home and now they were going to force us to evacuate I swallowed and hoped Jace would be able to make it here before we were forced to evacuate. I couldn't leave here without him. The thought of him getting here just to find out I'd already left, broke me. If that happened, the chance we'd find each other again was slim, especially with how often, and fast, they were moving people from sector to sector.

Running up the stairs, I burst through my door, half-hoping Jace would have made it to my window. But he hadn't. I crossed the room and lifted the window open, sticking my head out and breathing the cool night air. Jace wasn't waiting under the tree either. We still had a day and a half before I had to consider leaving without him.

Worry settled like a rock in my stomach as my thoughts

moved to him being found out in the middle of the crowd and captured.

Was the change of clothes enough for him to blend in? I had no doubt he would be treated as bad, or worse, than I had been.

Exhausted from my day, I pulled myself back in and glanced at the room, which felt strange to me after being away for so long. I wanted nothing more than to shower in my own bathroom and to wear my own clothes again.

I took my time with everything. Picking out my clothes slowly, running my hand along almost every piece I owned. I turned the shower on high. Steam enveloped the room within moments, fogging the mirror. I stepped inside and eased under the near scalding temperature. The water poured down my back, easing the aches and pains of my ordeal until they vanished and the water started to cool.

Pulling back the blankets of my bed, I crawled in, savoring each limited moment. It was such a contrast to what I'd had recently. My eyelids grew heavy, and I didn't fight it. There was only one thing missing that would have made it heaven.

A soft tapping on the window startled me fully awake. I shot out of bed and ran to open it. There was only one thing that sound could mean.

Jace hung on to a branch and looked at me with the same expression I knew was on my face.

"I was worried something would happen to you when that man took you from me," he whispered.

"How did you get away?" I asked, amazed to see him unharmed.

"I had to circle back toward the barricade and use the abandoned sectors to get around their evacuation."

Tears of relief prickled my eyes. I cupped his face and placed a kiss on his mouth.

"Get in here," I said, trying not to laugh. There was nothing funny about that moment, but the swirling emotions from seeing his face were playing havoc with me.

Jace stepped through the window and gathered me in his arms. Pulling me tight against him, one hand pressed my lower back to him and the other tangled itself in my hair. I fell into him without hesitation.

We kissed as if it were our last, and considering how fast the world had spun out of control, it was entirely possible it would be. Our passion began hot, the kisses desperate, hungry, and demanding. But the longer we held each other, the more they moved to illustrations of our feelings. Without words, we shared more than I ever thought possible.

He trailed his lips along my jaw and down my neck. I wrapped myself in him until we were a tangle of limbs as I tried to make us one so no one could ever separate us again.

"I love you, Jace," I whispered against his mouth.

"I love you, Raylinn." I could feel the tug of his lips as the corners turned up into a smile.

When we'd first met, I'd never thought my heart would

belong to him. Though the strong pull I'd felt had seemed like a brightly burning fire that would extinguish itself from burning too hot and too fast. But that fire had grown and changed. It hadn't cooled, but instead had grown stronger and more powerful, finding a fuel that would last forever.

We held each other tightly as we lay in the dark. It was a moment I would treasure always. I never wanted it to end. I let out a contented sigh.

"Are you—?"

"Shuush," I pressed a finger over his lips.

He tilted my chin up with a knuckle to meet his warm gaze. I missed the honeyed amber of his eyes. Even though I spent the better part of the last twenty-four hours with him, I hadn't taken the time to appreciate him as I'd wanted.

"What's wrong?" he asked quietly.

I took my time answering, trying to put what I was feeling into words.

"Sometimes, I think if I—if I just stay still long enough, then maybe I could stop time. Stop the world in its tracks and just listen to the silence. I try to imagine what it would be like if nothing outside this room changed."

"Lonely, I would think."

"No... I think it would be quiet and peaceful, and I could breathe without the meaningless pressures of arbitrary things. No schedules pushed on me, no one's expectations to live up to, and no judgments."

"What would you do with all your free time?" There was a lightness to his voice, as if he were half-teasing me.

"Nothing… everything. It doesn't matter. I could be anyone or anything. I could be myself without worry or consequence. But when I was ready, I could move again and restart time."

"And what moment would you pick to stop time?" he asked, though it was clear he already knew the answer. It was the same one he would pick if he could.

"This one; right here, right now."

He smiled lazily and pressed a soft kiss to my lips.

We didn't move for hours. I wanted to pretend I could stop time and delay the harsh light of morning, when we would have to return to the nightmare of reality. I fought sleep until it wrapped itself around me and pulled me into its embrace.

CHAPTER EIGHTEEN

A Questionable Plan

I stretched, trying to release the aches and tension from my body. Every inch was sore and exhaustion still clouded my mind. I could have lain there for days or weeks before I felt like myself again.

Jace's arm wrapped tighter around my waist, pulling me closer. He placed soft, lazy kisses on my neck and shoulders. His lips left a trail of heat that sent a shiver down my spine. I rolled over and buried my face in his chest.

"I wish we could stay like this forever," I murmured. "I just want to pretend that none of this is happening."

Jace stiffened next to me. The change in demeanor was so abrupt, that I pulled back and examined his face.

"What is it?" I asked. Lifting my hand, I ran it through his hair, pushing loose strands from his forehead.

A frown pulled at his lips. "I think it might be worse than anyone knows."

His words chilled me. I pushed myself up to sit. "What do you mean?"

"I've never seen a disease work as fast as this before. Something has been bothering me, but I couldn't put my finger on it until now." He sat up and faced me.

"You're killing me," I said. Suddenly, my insides were twisting themselves into knots. "What is it?"

"So far, I'd assumed this had been a human virus, but when I saw the dead Vor'onin, I knew it was something more but…" he hesitated. He averted his eyes. "I've never seen, or heard of, a virus that could infect and kill like this."

"This virus came on impossibly fast for us, and it's not just in this city, it's *everywhere* on earth," I said.

"It could be something completely different affecting us than the humans," he suggested.

"It's only been weeks, but if aliens are dying now too, wouldn't it make sense that it's the same?" I asked. "It seems too coincidental that two unknown viruses could attack within weeks."

Jace pushed the covers off and moved to the edge of the bed. He ran his fingers through his hair, then stood and crossed the room to the window. His hands gripped the edges that framed the glass as he stared out at something I couldn't see. "We had a virus once, centuries ago. It plagued our people, nearly killing us off. It was a slow and painful death."

I shivered and stood. I couldn't sit still while hearing about the thing that had ravaged his world. I joined him at the window.

"Jace? I thought you said your sun had died."

The space between us filled with an eerie quiet.

"It did, but there's more to it than I told you before." He kept his back to me as he spoke. "Our star was dying. Our scholars say the virus appeared after the temperatures rose. We don't know where it began. By the time we realized what was happening, it was too late."

Part of me wanted to run from the virus and everything that had to do with it. I started pacing the room. My muscles suddenly had so much more energy to burn.

I waited for him to continue.

"Some of the symptoms were a thinning and yellowing of the skin, insanity, and the breakdown of the lung tissue." He turned to face me. "The Vor'onin we came across seemed to have all of those symptoms. But it doesn't make sense. It takes a year to get to that point. If he were infected at all, his stasis pod never would have opened. This is too sudden to be the same thing."

I chewed on my nails, a habit I hadn't had since I was young. My teeth grazed the skin on my finger. I examined my nails. They were all down to the nubs. Apparently I'd been back at it longer than I'd realized.

"We called it Morelle, and it nearly wiped out my entire planet. A few were immune, and we were able to evacuate a few cities before it reached that far. Only a small handful of people out of millions were able to fight it. Though, as many studies as our scientists did, they could find nothing in those who were immune that differed from those who weren't."

"That's horrible…"

"Everyone who escaped, underwent an examination in a stasis pod for one year—the length of time it takes for it to invade the host until death."

A knock on the door made me jump. I paused and held my breath, wondering if whoever it was had heard Jace talking.

"Ray, breakfast is ready!" Mom called from the other side of the door. A second later, her footsteps on the wooden floor faded as she walked farther away.

I slumped in relief, honestly shocked with how often I'd had Jace in my room and still hadn't been caught.

"I should go," Jace said.

"Where will you go?"

He hesitated. "I'm not sure yet."

"Then stay with me, please?" I crossed the room and placed a hand on his arm. "When we leave here, I want you to go with us."

"How can I without your family knowing who I am?"

They would have to know. It would be impossible to bring him along without them finding out who and what he was. My gaze fell to the floor. I had an idea, and it was risky but…

"You can go out the window and wait for half an hour, then come to the front door." I reached up and adjusted the borrowed hoodie. Other than the bright amber eyes that twinkled down at me with the vertical pupils, Jace looked human. Any marks that identified him as Vor'on, were hidden under the outfit.

Jace moved to climb out the window.

"Hold on," I said.

As quietly as I could, I snuck into the hall. I could hear my parents and Mr. McCloy talking downstairs. I made my way across the hall to Toby's room. I snatched a hat off his dresser and hurried back to Jace.

I adjusted the hat over his head and stood back to admire my work, tapping my index finger against my lips. It was questionable, but it would have to do. Sunglasses inside would look suspicious.

"All right, you're ready. Just keep your head down and don't look anyone in the eye."

Jace stepped out the window, and I gave him one last kiss before he climbed down.

I waited until he disappeared around the corner before heading downstairs to face everyone.

The TV was on, but only snowy static filled the screen with the volume on low.

I made my way into the kitchen. My mother was busy cleaning, though everything already seemed cleaner than normal. My guess was that she was trying to keep busy.

"Morning," I said.

Toby looked up from a bowl of cereal. He stirred his food absentmindedly, but wasn't eating. He stifled a slight cough and quickly looked back down.

My hand went to my neck, and I flushed. I wondered if there was a telltale sign on me making it obvious I had guy in my room.

"Sit down," Mom said, walking over.

I sat and she placed a plate of eggs and slices of bacon in front of me. I shoveled the food into my mouth, and I didn't look up until I was nearly finished. My father and brother were both eating cereal. I had a feeling we were running low on food and she'd given me the last of the really good stuff. I felt guilty for inhaling most of it before realizing.

At least Fred wasn't around, making my home feel like home. I must have missed him after I'd grabbed the hat from Toby's room.

"Where's Mr. McCloy?" I asked between bites, hoping they'd say he had left.

"I was outside smoking." I cringed as he walked back into the room. He stopped just inside the kitchen doorway.

Toby coughed and everyone froze.

"If you're getting sick, we need to call it in," Fred spoke. He said it as if it were a routine thing we'd all lived with our entire lives, as if the meaning of calling it in meant nothing.

Immediately, anger boiled within my veins. I didn't even think. I slammed my fork on the table and glared at the man who had come into my life and tried to take charge of everything.

This wasn't his family. This wasn't his son or brother he was talking about. This was *my* brother. My pain in the butt brother who gave me a hard time any chance he got.

"He just choked on a bite of food," I snapped. "Just because there's a virus doesn't mean you get to turn my family in for eating."

My dad placed a hand over mine. With my excuse, Toby didn't hold back, and the coughing fit sounded loud in the otherwise silent room. It resonated deep in his chest, and even I knew the truth. He hadn't choked on his food. He hadn't even taken a bite the entire time I'd been in the room.

"Toby is fine," Dad said. He folded his paper and gave Toby a look.

A glass crashed and shattered.

"Oh, how clumsy," my mother muttered with an audible tremor in her voice. I glanced at her between the men. She was a nervous wreck. Her hands shook as she scrambled to pick up the broken glass.

"We need to be cautious about this. The virus is highly contagious, and I don't think I need to remind you of that, Michael. It would be better to call now than risk infecting everyone else here."

"You are a guest in this house," Dad reminded him. "You don't decide anything when it comes to my family."

"It's a federal offense, and it puts us all at risk."

They spoke in conversational tones, but the tension from their battle of wills was suffocating. My gaze went between Toby and my dad. Guilt was all over Toby's face, and he didn't turn once to look at Mr. McCloy. I wanted to just reach out and tell him it would be okay, that our parents would take care of him, but I stayed in my seat.

"This is *my* family." I'd never heard Dad speak with such anger before. His face was red as his blood pressure visibly rose. "If I think my son is sick with the virus, then *I* will call the CDC. But until then, leave it be."

"I heard coughing during the night," Mr. McCloy insisted.

Why won't this man drop it already? I gritted my teeth, knowing whatever I said wouldn't help.

"You worry too much, Fred. No one else here is sick. If he had the virus, we'd all have it," my mother said, trying to soothe them. "If anything, it's only a head cold from the stress of everything going on; you know he's always had stress colds."

"Then it shouldn't be a problem for the CDC to check him out and clear him." Fred narrowed his blue eyes on Toby, who was doing his best to avoid the conversation.

"You're not in the military anymore, Fred. You don't have any authority here," my dad continued. "We let you stay, but you are free to leave if you don't agree with how I run my household."

"It's not worth any of our lives to protect one person. It's an unnecessary risk," Fred said.

"He's not just one person, he is *my son!*" Dad shouted. He'd finally reached his snapping point. His hands slammed on the table as he pushed himself up. "And you know damn well that no one who's shown signs of anything and been taken to quarantine has ever made it out alive."

The man who'd implanted himself in our lives looked at each of us in turn, daring us to question the jurisdiction he seemed to think he had. "You need to be objective about this."

Fred crossed from the doorway, where he'd been standing the whole time, and pulled Toby back by the shoulder.

"Hey, what—" Toby objected as he was treated like nothing more than a child.

"I need to check you out." Fred tilted Toby's chin back and looked into his eyes. I don't know what he saw, or if he was even qualified to make an assessment that could damn my brother to a quarantine he would never make it out of.

"Get off me." Toby tried to twist out of Fred's grasp. It didn't seem to matter. Whatever so-called symptoms Fred was looking for, he had already decided.

"He's sick," Mr. McCloy announced. "We can't take the chance he won't become one of the ones that turn into runners rather than just die."

His words were so cold. I wanted to slap the smug expression off his face. This man wasn't a doctor; he wasn't qualified to make that call.

"Get. Out." My dad spoke slowly through gritted teeth, punctuating both words.

Mr. McCloy looked from my brother to Dad, and frowned as if he didn't understand what the issue was.

"I said, *get out.* Now!" Dad hollered. His balled up fists supported his weight as he leaned on the table. He looked like he was ready to punch him.

"Fine, but I'm not about to let you infect me and possibly thousands of others just to keep your son out of quarantine."

Then the man I'd come to dislike—no, hate—within just minutes of being around him, regardless of his good intentions, finally left with the front door slamming shut behind him. While it was a relief to have him out of our house, dread still filled my stomach like a ton of rocks.

I looked from my brother to my mom, then to my dad. We all wore the same expression of shock and worry, and we were all speechless.

My father found his voice first. "We leave in an hour," he said.

CHAPTER NINETEEN

Edge of Sanity

"I suggest you all go pack what you need. We need to get out of here and find somewhere safe to go until Toby's better, before the CDC shows up."

"Are you sure he'll call them?" Mom asked, wringing her hands.

"I have no doubt about it." Dad moved around the table toward the door. "Sharon, if we have any cold medicine or cough drops, grab them. I'll go get our bags."

The clock on the stove said eight forty-seven. Only about twenty minutes had passed since I'd gone downstairs. While I wanted to be here when Jace showed up, I didn't have an excuse just to stand there for the next ten minutes.

Begrudgingly, I went upstairs. Toby followed close behind. He cleared his throat in an attempt not to cough. I couldn't imagine what he was feeling in that moment.

Grabbing a bag from my room, I shoved a few changes of clothes in my bag while still keeping some room for last minute things.

I did a quick scan of my room, of everything I would be leaving everything behind. I had to leave all of my pictures and memories behind, possibly for some random person to find and use while they tried to avoid catching the virus, or just as bad, runners attacking them. I wanted to hope we could return, but the likelihood of that just didn't seem possible.

My eyes landed on a framed picture of Miranda and me from the homecoming dance freshman year. We wore large smiles and our futures were full of endless possibilities.

Now, everything had changed. We had no idea what the future would hold—if there even was a future waiting, or if it had been stolen from us in the matter of a few, short weeks.

A knock on the door jolted me out of my thoughts. I set the picture down, grabbed my bag, and raced down the stairs. I got to the door breathless at the same time as my dad, earning a strange look from him.

Toby coughed from the top of the stairs. He looked nervous. Then it hit me—*it might not be Jace at the door.*

Dad waved Toby back before opening the door. He frowned and didn't say anything for a long moment. I peeked around the door and was relieved to see it was Jace.

"Jace," I said, pushing past my dad to open the door wider. "Come in."

"You know this boy?" Dad asked.

"Yeah, he goes to my school."

"Ray, he needs to go," my dad said. "We're in the middle of something."

"No, he can't, I—" At a loss for words, I looked to Jace.

Toby was racked with a coughing fit loud enough to be heard through his door. I rubbed my chest with a hand absentmindedly, trying to ease the pain I knew he felt.

"We can trust him," I said, looking my father in the eye. "Just give me a minute to talk to him, okay?"

His face said he clearly wasn't happy about it, but he walked away without saying anything.

I took Jace's hand and led him to the couch.

"Jace," I whispered after making sure we were alone. "I think Toby's sick. Is there any chance there's a cure?"

"I don't know. We'd have to go back to the ship to check. I don't think that it's a good—"

"Please, Jace? He's my brother. I can't let anything happen to him. Not if I can help him. When you got me away from Lar'ruk, I think he was about to tell me something. He knew things about us, but he wasn't going to tell Thral'el. I think he would be willing to help us." It was selfish of me to ask him to risk his life, again. But I had to help Toby.

He dropped his chin, resigned to do what I asked of him. "I think the testing Doctor Lar'ruk was doing on humans was to find a cure. I don't know if he succeeded. He might not have even been close. He never mentioned it to anyone, so I can't be sure."

"Will you go with me then?" I asked. I wouldn't blame him if he said no, not after what had happened last time.

"There's a chance they'll lock you up again," he warned.

"What if we don't enter the ship? They can't just kidnap me if I'm not inside, right?"

Jace didn't look pleased with the idea, but none-the-less, he agreed. "Yes, I will go with you."

"Thank you so much!" I threw my arms around his neck and placed a kiss on his cheek. My heart felt lighter at knowing I didn't have to sit and wait for the worst to happen. I no longer felt powerless, and I think Jace understood. There was just one more thing we needed to do before we could leave.

Jace smiled wryly.

"Do you trust me?" I asked.

His smile slipped. "Yes."

I took a deep breath and stood to adjust Jace's cap. I turned and called out, "Mom, Dad, Toby! Can you come here for a moment?"

"What it is Ray?" Dad asked, rushing into the room with Mom close behind.

"I'll explain when Toby's here."

A few minutes later, Toby finally joined us. The whole time he looked at Jace with an odd expression as he sat on the couch next to him. "Hey, is that my—"

I punched him lightly in the shoulder. He didn't say anything more, but he looked from the hat to me and back as if slowly putting it together.

Now that everyone was sitting and waiting on me for answers, I was suddenly nervous.

"Uh, look," I started, then cleared my throat. "I know Toby is sick."

Toby paled, visibly shaken. Mom shook her head and gripped my dad's hand tightly.

"Ray!" Dad admonished.

"It's okay, Dad." I looked from him to Jace. I bit down hard on the inside of my cheek. "Jace won't tell anyone, we can trust him... In fact, he said there is a very, *very*, small chance there might-be-a-cure." The last few words rushed from me before I could take them back.

"What?" Mom asked. "A cure? Is that possible?"

"I-I don't know for sure. The thing is... we'd have to go look. But there *is* a slight chance."

"How would he know if there's a cure?" Toby asked.

"Yeah, about that..." I gripped the top of my hair in my fist, not sure how to tell them the next part. I looked to Jace standing silently next to me, his gaze firmly on the ground. "He knows the doctor who might have been working on one."

"Ray, no doctors have had a chance to start the research with how fast it's come on. It's all they can do to keep it contained."

I sighed. "It's complicated."

"What are you telling us, Ray?" Toby demanded.

"None of *our* doctors have been working on it." I let that sink in for a moment.

"You mean, he's been working with the Others?" Dad asked.

"The Vor'onins, yeah, because he… is… one."

"Excuse me?" Toby stood up and grabbed me by the shoulders, forcing me to look him in the eye. "What are you saying, Ray?"

I pulled away. "I'm saying Jace is Vor'on." All three of their faces stared at me with blank, confused expressions. "An Other—alien—whatever, he's one of them."

By the time I finished speaking, I was standing in front of him, using my body to shield him.

Jace placed a hand on my shoulder and stepped forward. He took off Toby's hat and looked them all in the eye, one by one, letting them see his amber eyes and elongated pupils. His hand reached up and tugged on the collar of his hoodie, exposing the three scar-like lines on his neck.

"So that *is* my hat!" Toby nearly shouted.

"Look," I said. "We can trust him. I promise. *He's* the reason I was able to get back here from… quarantine. Mr. McCoy saw me two sectors away and dragged me here even though I was already on my way home. He didn't save me from anything,

Jace did."

"Oh, thank you!" Mom shot up from the couch and hugged Jace tightly. She could have been thanking him for making sure I was safe, or for giving us hope about a cure, or both.

"If there's a cure, how will we get it?" my dad asked.

"You're not going to like this, but Jace and I have to go to his ship. His doctor had been doing research on the infected since the first sign of the virus. So if there is a cure, that's where it will be."

"No, you are not going across the city. Not through the cut off sectors of infected, that's too far. I'll go with him."

"Dad, trust me, please. I have to do this. You have to take care of Mom and keep Toby safe until we come back. It's the only hope we have of saving him."

"I don't like this." Mom was wringing her hands and looking between Jace and me.

"We'll be back soon. Besides, Jace knows his way around the barricades. We'll meet you in a day and a half. But we need to go now, and you have to go now too, before Mr. McCloy brings people back for Toby."

I looked down at him, realizing he'd been quiet. He was sitting on the couch staring blankly ahead.

"You have a day and a half, get back sooner if you can," Dad said reluctantly. "Meet us at your friend, Miranda's house. It's taken them three to five days to move sectors, that should give you enough time to get back."

I knew it was hard for him to let me walk into a dangerous situation, but it was this, or risk being put into quarantine together with the infected running around. None of us would last long even if Toby wasn't sick.

I gave everyone a hug and a kiss on the cheek. I hated leaving them, but I *had* to save my brother. I had to try anyway. Barely fighting back the tears of emotion, I threw some small energy bars in my bag and left out the back door with Jace.

Jace was quiet as we moved through the alleys and between houses. It was slow progress going through my sector and the next. We still had all day. The sun was both a blessing and a curse. It was easier to be spotted, and we were clearly going places we shouldn't. At least we could see any military personnel or runners from a greater distance than at night.

We didn't pause until we were out of the sectors still populated with people.

"What you're doing is brave, Raylinn," Jace said. It wasn't until he pulled me into a hug that I realized how close to tears I had been this entire time. I let him hold me for a moment, trying to convince myself he was right. That what I was doing for my family was brave, even though all I wanted to do was to curl up in a ball and hide. This wasn't a choice for me. I wasn't choosing to be "brave." I was doing this because that's what you do for the people you love.

I pulled away. "Let's go, we need to hurry before Toby gets worse."

We continued to run through the sectors, taking slightly different paths than before. Hours went by, my feet began to ache, and my legs grew tired.

"We should rest for a while," Jace said. He must have noticed how much I'd slowed down.

"No, we should keep—"

"We won't make it if you're too exhausted to even walk on the way back. Rest for a little bit now, and we will be able to move faster."

"Yeah, but… in an alley?" I said, looking around. We were crossing through the center of the downtown area, and he'd chosen to stop in a narrow alley behind a few local shops. Dumpsters dotted the brick walls and grease, which had spilled all over the pavement, gave the area a rancid smell.

I found a narrow stoop at the back door of a restaurant and sat down. It was the only semi-clean spot. The brick of the building was rough, tugging at strands of my hair as I leaned my head against it and tried to relax. The sky was beginning to change from bright blue to the deeper shades mixed with purples and pinks.

I'd been half-asleep when a glass bottle skittered across the pavement, making me jump.

Jace whirled around and took a step back. "Raylinn… stay behind me."

I shot to my feet and looked down the way we had come. A man stumbled, as if drunk, pausing when he spotted Jace. He lifted his head and sniffed the air, much like a dog would. In a flash, he was running towards us.

"Run!" Jace said, shoving me in the opposite direction. I hesitated, not wanting to leave him. "I can't fight him if you're near me. I'll be too worried about you."

I waited another beat before moving. I hit the end of the alley and skidded to a stop. I barely had half a chance to look at my surroundings before I was tackled to the ground.

My head hit the cement hard. Stars exploded in my vision as the rough concrete scraped my arm. Something sounded like a cross between a growl and a moan from above me made my heart pound so hard I thought it would explode.

I flailed, kicking and punching. My fist connected with a face, and I felt a slight crunch. I couldn't tell if it was my hand, or the face it had come in contact with. But it was enough to give me room to scramble to my feet. I ran with no destination in mind, just trying to get as far away as I could.

After a few blocks, I turned to look over my shoulder. A woman, with a discolored, blueish face, ran after me. I pushed myself to run harder.

The wind was knocked out of me as I crashed into someone. Panicking had made me careless. I stumbled back, prepared to tell them to run. Clouded eyes, unseeing, stared back as blood dribbled down the chin of the teen boy who sniffed the air in front of me.

I swore under my breath and changed directions. My lungs

ached, and I could feel my legs begin to lose speed the longer I ran. Gulping in large breaths, I knew I wouldn't last much longer.

"Ahhhhhhh!" I heard a cry, then the clank of a metal object hitting a solid mass.

I changed direction again to give me a better view of what had happened, not daring to slow.

A man with facial scruff and dirty, wrinkled clothes swung a metal pipe at the woman. Her body jerked back and she stumbled, giving him an opening to take a swing at the teen before she recovered. The longer he fought them, the closer they inched forward. Closer and closer, threatening to overtake him.

I couldn't just run off and let this man fight them alone. I turned toward him and ran. I didn't know how I could help. Distraction, so he could disable one enough to keep it from coming after us, was the best plan I could come up with.

He raised his arms, holding the pipe like an ax. The metal came down hard on the teen's head. The hit should have knocked him out cold, but the boy wasn't even fazed. He lifted his arms again, but the woman grabbed hold of one arm.

She hardly seemed to use any effort as she redirected his movements, bringing her face down to meet his flesh. She bit down hard and he screamed.

Blood oozed from the wound as she continued to bite. It dripped down his arm and poured to the ground in a waterfall of crimson.

So much blood...

I stopped several yards away and fell to my knees as my breakfast rebelled against the sight. I lost it right there.

When I looked up, the teen was on him too.

"Hey!" I yelled out of instinct. It was pretty stupid, considering I didn't have a plan, and I'd just wretched up the entire contents of my stomach. The man had dropped the metal pipe. I started toward them, intent on helping him.

"Run!" the man bellowed, stopping me from coming to his aid.

Tears stung my eyes before falling down my cheeks in burning rivulets.

Run. Everyone was always telling me to run. I knew I couldn't save him. I knew that even if I could beat them off, he'd die in minutes from his injuries. The boy had the man's abdomen exposed and was clawing at it, causing more blood to flow.

The scruffy man who had saved me, lay still.

Guilt rose in the form of bile once again.

Chapter Twenty

A Silent Scream

"Raylinn!" Jace skidded to a stop at my side.

"I-I can't help him," I muttered. My mind clouded over in shock.

"Don't let his sacrifice be in vain."

"But… why? Why did he do it?"

"I don't know." Jace pulled me up by my arm and grabbed my face in both hands, forcing me to look him in the eyes. "We have to run, remember why we are going to the ship. We need to help your brother."

His words snapped me out of it.

"Okay, okay," I said, more to myself than him.

Jace kept his hand on my upper back to keep me from looking back and slowing us down. We started at a walk as I tried to work the overabundance of adrenaline out of my system. I could feel the urgency in the pressure of his hand, and I sped up as soon as my legs felt steady enough. Leaving behind all the horrible things those monsters did to the man who gave his life to save me lent speed to my steps.

We crossed through to the next sector as quickly as we could, finding the edge of the next, and crossing at an angle to put distance between the runners and us.

The sun had just fallen below the horizon when we made it to the edge of the park. Some of the ships were open, but all the lights were off. The hum of machinery I'd grown used to hearing as we approached the park was missing, leaving the usual silence of the night to give an eerie feel. We crossed through the grassy area to the center ship.

Like many of the others, it too was open.

"Jace?" I whispered. Though I tried to speak as quietly as possible, it still sounded loud to my ears. "What happened?"

He approached the ship, quietly ascending the steps and entering. I backed into the shadow of another ship. My heel caught on something and I fell, landing on my back. I sat up, rubbing my head and squinting into the darkness to see what I'd tripped over. My hand shot to my mouth, barely containing the shriek ripping its way free.

Jace was at my side in an instant. "What happened? Are you okay?"

I shook all over, afraid if I opened my mouth to speak, I would end up screaming instead. I pointed a trembling finger at the alien's body.

Jace's jaw clenched. "Come with me," he said, helping me up. "But… it's not any better in the ship. Prepare yourself."

I swallowed hard, wondering if my mind could take what I was about to walk into. *For Toby,* I reminded myself as I followed a few steps behind.

Even after everything I'd seen today, I still hadn't expected the carnage that awaited us as we stepped inside. Dim lights flickered on overhead at our entrance. Dozens of bodies lay everywhere, blood soaked the floors and walls. The smell of already rotting flesh permitted the air. I covered my nose with the inside of my shirt, trying my hardest to breathe through my mouth instead. It was a minute before I realized the bodies belonged to both Vor'onins and humans alike.

There had been a war inside this ship, horrible and grotesque. Their weapons of choice had been teeth and nails. Chunks of flesh were missing in most of the bodies. Some of the humans had scorch marks marring their skin. I turned away, unable to look another second.

"Jace…" I pleaded.

"Let's see if there's anyone left alive."

I let him lead the way, keeping my eyes trained on his back as we made our way down the same hall we had during my first visit.

"It's okay now," he said after a few moments, pausing in a side hall. "I want to see if any of the elders, or Thral'el made it. You can wait here if you—"

"No," I said firmly. I didn't want to see any more carnage, but I felt safer at his side.

We walked down the passage and ended up in the room where my trial had been held. Dark forms sprawled on the floor, and I turned my face away as the lights flickered to life.

Jace muttered something under his breath and slammed a fist against the wall.

"I'm so sorry, Jace."

I held no love for them, but that didn't diminish the fact that they were Jace's people—his family. And he'd lost them all. This ship was all that was left of his home world. His father lay among the bodies. I didn't know if he recognized him. I wasn't sure if it would make it better or worse.

Jace spun on his heel away from the slaughter and strode back the way we'd come. "Let's go. There's nothing we can do now," he said through clenched teeth. "The entire council is dead."

I had to jog to keep up with his long strides. I hated what his people had done to me when I was here, but I never wanted this for Jace, or them. No one deserved that.

We were nearing the storage and lab area when he stopped at a narrow door and pushed it open. Quickly, he let it close and moved on.

I didn't want to ask, but I had to know. "Jace, what was in there?"

"Char'ra didn't make it. She was infected and chained herself to her dais."

So far there had been no survivors, but perhaps the doctor in his room —

Bright light flashed before my eyes and the breath was sucked from my lungs. I froze, gasping for air. The feel of needles penetrated my arms, legs, and chest. My hands clumsily grasped at my body, trying to pull the needles from my skin. My body couldn't move—I was being held down.

No, no, no! Not again! I wanted to scream, but no sound came out.

"Ray? Raylinn? What's wrong?"

I heard the words, felt the weight of his hands on my arms, and focused. Slowly, the pain faded. I blinked up into Jace's face. Looking around, I realized I wasn't in the chair being treated like a science experiment.

Finally catching my breath, I rubbed my face. "I think... I think I had a panic attack."

"Are you okay to continue? You can wait here if you need to."

Toby.

"I'm fine, let's go."

Toby, Toby, Toby. I chanted his name in my mind as we approached, then entered the lab. His name kept my mind focused and my feet moving forward.

I stood on the edge just inside. The lab was in disarray... papers scattered, vials knocked over and shattered. I dropped my bag near the door and walked further in. Each step a painful reminder of my so-called examination.

A rasping sound set my skin to crawling. I looked around trying to find the source. An arm peeked out from around a corner toward where the shower was. I made my way over, hoping the limb was still attached to someone.

Taking a deep breath, I forced myself to look. The doctor lay on the ground, his breath ragged and shuttering.

"Jace! The doctor, he's still alive."

Jace dashed across the lab and was at the doctor's side in a blink. "He's badly injured. I can't move him to the stasis pod…"

As much as I hated the doctor for treating me the way he had when he had controlled me, I knelt next to Jace and placed a hand on his shoulder. We'd left and everyone had been alive, and now, this horrible doctor was the last living being Jace had from his world.

"Is there a cure?" Jace demanded.

Doctor Lur'ruk opened and closed his mouth without speaking.

"Tell me! If there's a cure, where is it?"

"There issss…" The word trailed off.

Jace looked up at me with sorrowful eyes.

"Damn it!" I cried. We had been so close to knowing if there was a cure. Now we had nothing but a ransacked lab. I grabbed the doctor by his shirt. "Is there a cure? Where is it?" I yelled as I shook him.

His chest shuttered and slowed before stopping. I let go, letting him slump back to the ground.

I pushed myself to my feet and stumbled into the main lab,

half blinded by tears. I leaned on a counter and let it support me. My heart demanded I lash out, destroy everything, and it took every ounce of restraint I possessed just to keep from letting my anger get the best of me.

My legs shook and I slid to the ground as fresh tears fell. I wrapped my arms around my knees, pulling them tight against my chest, and buried my face. My short fingernails gripped my arms so tightly they dug into my flesh.

I stayed like that until I'd cried out the frustration and pain that had nowhere else to go, and my breathing had evened out.

The sound of glass clinking softly drew me from the bubble I had created. Jace was moving around the lab, looking through the unbroken vials and reading labels.

He hadn't given up.

I wiped my sleeves over my face, ashamed it had taken so little to get me to become useless. I stood and started on the opposite side of the room.

Picking up an unbroken vial, I realized all the writing was in the Vor'onin script. I set it back down and started clearing out the broken glass with a cloth that had been sitting next to the sink. I worked quickly, trying to get rid of anything that would make his search all the more difficult.

When I finished, I grabbed files and charts that had been scattered, placing them in a neat pile.

Resting my hand on top of the stack, I looked to Jace. His hair was messy and his shoulders had lost the rigidity they'd held when I had first met him. Dark circles were under his eyes, but he was still just as attractive as ever, even despite his own exhaustion. If I didn't know better, I'd say he was human. I wonder if he felt the same when he looked at me, did he see someone not so different from himself?

Jace cleared his throat.

"I found a stack of folders, I think they are charts, but I don't know what they say. I can't read—" I picked up a paper with hundreds of symbols and waved finger at it, "—this."

He pushed the last tray of vials away and stood next to me. Jace flipped through the files, sorting them into piles.

"Why are you separating them into different stacks?" I asked. *This would go a lot faster if I could read the language.*

Jace paused on one file. His hands crinkled the paper as his face contorted in anger. He ripped it to shreds and threw them onto the ground. I took a step back, shocked by the uncharacteristic outburst.

"What was that?" I asked breathlessly.

His chest heaved as he fought to control himself again. "That was your file."

"You broke me out before he could do anything serious to me," I said, placing a hand on his arm.

"You don't know the things he would have done to you."

I swallowed. If Jace was that upset, then it had to be bad. A shiver raced down my spine, freezing my blood at the fate I had almost had.

"It's okay. He can't do them now." I tried to add confidence to my words, but it sounded fake even to my ears.

Jace pulled in a deep breath then let it out slowly. He pointed to the tall stack, then the short. "I'm separating them into subject files and notes."

I picked through the pile he'd indicated as notes, looking for anything that stood out. Most pages had hundreds of symbols. Though the symbols were beautiful, they left me wondering how they could read it, even knowing what each one meant.

One page caught my attention. The writing was bold and large. Rather than a page covered like the rest were, there were only a few lines of symbols on this one.

"Jace, what does this say?" I asked. I brushed my fingers over the symbols I'd only seen the last time I was on the ship.

"It says there's no cure, it didn't bond."

The crack of my heart breaking in my chest was almost audible. My family was counting on me to find a cure. I'd promised I'd bring one home for Toby. Though they had known it was never a certainty, guilt still raged within me.

"Hmm," Jace was looking at the page with a furrowed brow and pursed lips. One hand absentmindedly rubbed his chin. Not the expression I had expected after discovering just how hopeless our mission had been.

"What?" I leaned over his shoulder, trying to see what he was looking at.

"Well, you see how this symbol has an extra swoop?" He pointed to it as if I would actually recognize it. Part of me wanted to laugh, but I knew he was just focused. "It looks like the symbol that indicates up."

"I don't understand," I said, picking up another sheet of notes. This one also had less than the others did.

"It's strange. All the other notes of his I've seen were immaculate, so why not this one?"

"Do you think he was trying to tell you something? That there was a cure after all?" I could hardly dare to hope, but against all logic, my heart grabbed onto it and held tight.

There was a long, nerve-wracking silence as he continued to study the notes intently. "I'm not sure. Doctor Lar'ruk did have some methods most of the elder council questioned from time to time, but I never knew any of the specifics of the tensions between them."

I twisted my hands together.

"He often questioned the motives and wisdom of the council."

"Do you think he was hiding the cure from them?" I held my breath.

"I was going to begin an apprenticeship with him in two cycles," he said, finally looking up from the page.

My mouth hung open.

Jace. My *Jace was planning on working with the man who had tortured me? Could I really love someone who was okay with treating anyone like that?*

Chapter Twenty-One

A Nice Dream

"You were going to work with him?" I spat the words.

Jace lifted his head. The confused, almost innocent, expression angered me even though the logical part of my brain knew his reaction was normal in that situation.

"You were going to work with the *doctor*," I lifted my hands to make air quotes as I said the word doctor, "who was going to use me as a lab rat and possibly torture me to death?"

"Raylinn, I never would have let him do any of that to you. I promised I would keep you safe."

I rested my elbows on the table and pressed my forehead into my palms. "I'm sorry, I just can't stand thinking about what he did to me... what he was going to do. I know I said it was okay, but it's not. And when you said—"

He wrapped his arms around me and pulled me to his chest. "You don't have to explain, I understand."

I took several breaths, focusing on why we were there. Exhaustion and stress had worn my body down with each passing hour. In such a short time, I'd pushed myself beyond all my limits, both physically and mentally, and my emotions were all over the place.

"Let's keep looking; I have to save Toby," I said, pulling away.

We fell into silence as we looked for anything that stuck out. I still had no clue what to look for, other than inconsistencies. Part of me felt hopeless, like we were just wasting time.

I stopped and examined a sheet that only had a few messy notes scrawled across it. "What about this?" I asked.

He took the paper and turned it around.

"These notes don't make any sense," he said. "My best guess is that he thinks the virus has something in common with the Morelle virus, or—"

"Or? Or what Jace?" I dropped the page I'd just picked up.

"Or that it might be a variation of the virus."

"But how? From everything you've told me, anyone carrying the virus would never have been released from those pod things."

"If it is the virus, then it was knowingly carried aboard." He paced the floor as he read the notes over and over, looking for answers he knew weren't there. "But why would Thral'el, or

Doctor Lar'ruk, bring it when we had worked so hard to leave all traces behind? People we sacrificed. Anyone in a stasis pod who had the virus, were supposed to be left on Vor'on. What were they doing with it on board?"

Slowly, the meaning of what he said clicked into place, forming a picture. "You mean they *knowingly* brought it here? They unleashed it on us? They are responsible for the countless deaths, the horror of everything that's happened?" With each word, my voice rose higher and higher until I was screaming. "Why?" I demanded, my throat raw.

I threw the papers in my hand and they fluttered to the floor, landing among the other various debris, but I didn't care. I paced the room like a wild animal ready to attack.

"My brother is going to die because they brought it here! They were going to kill me, they've already killed countless people—" my voice cracked.

I grabbed a tray of vials and threw them at the wall, but it did nothing to satisfy the rage boiling within me. I smashed my fist against the thick glass wall over and over until I collapsed on the floor again. Hot tears rolled down my face. Everything I knew, and everyone I loved, was being destroyed. And I had no idea why.

Broken glass cut into my knees and hands as I sobbed.

An invasion? But they didn't need to do this—they had the technology to get rid of us without this mess. But if this had been their plan, an attempt for us to go quietly, then they didn't get away unscathed. It had backfired and they were suffering as we were.

Jace knelt beside me.

I wanted to blame him as I'd blamed the rest of the Vor'onins, but I couldn't. He was just finding this out at the same time as I was; he was suffering the same as me.

His arm stiffened. He let go and moved around me.

"Excuse me," Jace said, leaning me to the side. His focus entirely on what he saw.

The unexpected response made me pause. I sniffled and moved out of the way, watching him carefully open a lower cabinet with a broken lock.

Jace pushed some dark bottles to the side and reached further back. Slowly, he brought his hand out, clutching a vile filled with a thick blue liquid sloshing around inside.

"What is that?" I asked.

"I'm not sure; it doesn't have a label on it. But it was pushed to the back."

Something in the back of my mind nagged at me. I was trying to think over everything we had learned, separating it from the overwhelming emotions.

"You said the weird squiggly was the symbol for up. So, what if that meant something?"

"What do you mean?" Jace asked. For the first time since we'd met, he looked worn down. *Almost entirely human.* It wasn't the bags under his eyes I'd seen earlier, it was more than that. His skin was paler than usual too. He almost didn't look like himself.

I shook my head trying to clear my thoughts. "What if, it meant there was no cure above? The stack it was in was on the counter. If Doctor Lar'ruk didn't want the elder council to know there was a cure then that would explain why it was hidden."

I could have been reaching, but it was a chance I was willing to take.

"It is strange it wasn't with any of the other filled vials," he admitted.

"Do you think it could be the cure?" I'd sat up and gripped the arm holding the blue liquid. My gaze focused on the liquid in the vial within his hand, willing it to be the cure we desperately needed.

"If there is a cure in this room," he spoke slowly, testing his words. "Then this would most likely be it."

I stood, dragging him up with me. "Jace, we have to go now!"

"But Rayli—" he started.

"We can't waste any more time. I don't know how bad Toby is and…"

"Raylinn, we don't know for sure. It might be something else entirely."

I stopped, dropping my gaze to the floor. It was all I could do to keep a fresh wave of tears at bay. "I know it might not be it. But there's nothing else in here that is even remotely close to it. If it is the cure, then we can save Toby, if not…" I shuttered. "Then at least we tried."

Jace hung his head. "Very well. We'll try it."

I picked my bag up from the floor and turned back to him. His hand was outstretched, offering me the vial.

"In case we get separated again, you stand a better chance making it back to your family than I would."

I nodded.

We ran through the ship, speeding up as we neared the entrance. The sickly smell of decaying flesh was stronger than it had been a few hours ago.

Once we were back on the ground, I inhaled a large breath of fresh air. It was cool on my face, and after being inside the ship, it was sweet and heavy with the fragrance of spring. The moon hung heavy in the sky, but it did nothing to dull the glitter of the Milky Way as it stretched out above in a sparkling ribbon.

"Jace, I…" I was interrupted by a long exaggerated yawn. "I need to rest soon. I don't know if I can make it." I hated admitting it, and the thought of wasting more time made me sick to my stomach, but if I didn't stop soon, I'd collapse before we even made it halfway home. Never mind the extra few miles to Miranda's house.

"There is an abandoned sector nearby; we can rest at one of the domiciles for a few hours."

"Perfect," I sighed.

I followed, jogging behind him. His definition of nearby was different than mine. Twenty minutes later, or an hour, or two—I couldn't tell how much time had passed, I'd zoned out for a while—we finally entered the edge of a neighborhood.

Jace found a house with an open door, and we walked in as quietly as we could. It gave me the creeps walking into a strange house in the middle of the night. It was almost enough to make me push through the exhaustion. I waited just inside the door while he checked the house for anyone or anything that might have been lingering.

He walked back down the stairs, his face lit only by the light of the moon shining through the window.

"All clear," Jace said.

I moved into the living room and plopped down on the couch. It was lumpy and not at all comfortable. *Did people live here, or was this house just for show?* I grumbled inwardly.

Jace sat at the far end of the couch and lifted my legs onto his lap.

"Wake me in a few hours, we should try to... get moving before dawn," I mumbled as I drifted off to sleep, my words punctuated by another yawn.

I woke to the feeling of fire burning my throat. It was as if I'd swallowed glass, then gargled with lemons. A coughing fit shook my body. I pushed myself to a sitting position while I waited for the spasms to subside. I couldn't remember the last time I'd had a drink of water.

Rubbing my chest, I looked out the window. Panic filled my veins. Pink colored the edge of the horizon as the sky slowly began to chase the darkness away. I quickly glanced to Jace, who must have fallen asleep as well. It was morning and we'd slept too long. He blinked wearily, shaking off the last traces of a deep sleep.

"I'm sorry," he croaked. "I must have been more tired than I realized."

We'd wasted a lot of time… but I couldn't blame him. We'd run for what felt like days with little to no rest. We were wearing ourselves out.

"It's okay, we needed the rest," I said. There was no use dwelling on it.

Our pace was sluggish as we cut across the first sector. I found it hard to keep putting one foot in front of the other. My energy was lacking to the point that I felt as if the sleep had drained me rather than replenish my much-needed energy. I tried to shake it off, forcing myself to move faster.

I reached into my bag as I jogged, pulling out an energy bar. I offered one to Jace, but he waved it off. Each bite was like a million tiny knives slicing at my throat as I swallowed.

What I wouldn't give for a glass of ice-cold water. I was pushing every part of myself to the limit.

We neared the shopping center down town, where the scruffy

man had saved me. I tried not to think about it, but found it impossible to ignore as Jace continued to lead us in that direction.

"Jace," I panted. "We should go a different way."

He slowed his pace enough for me to catch up. "This is the fastest route."

"I-I know, but I just don't want to see… the man's body."

"We can go around, but it will take more time," Jace offered. His brows drew together.

So selfish, I chastised myself. My brother was *dying* and all I could think about was myself.

"No, forget it. I'll be fine." I pushed my legs harder, willing them to take larger, faster strides.

As we neared the area, I tried to keep my eyes toward the horizon and the back of Jace's head.

We skirted around his body by a few yards, but as hard as I'd tried to avoid the sight, my gaze was still drawn to him like a magnet.

Unwillingly, I turned my head. His foot twitched. His hand.

I stopped jogging.

"Oh my God, Jace. He's still *alive!* We have to help him."

"Raylinn, that's not a good idea," he protested, but I ignored him.

I approached, slowing as I neared. His injuries looked extensive. But I thought that if he were alive, then I might be able to help, even if it was only a comforting hand.

"Sir? Are you—" I placed a hand on his shoulder, the only

unbloodied spot I could see. His chin jerked stiffly toward my voice. Clouded eyes set in a pale, gaunt face stared through me. An arm, with bone protruding from the skin, wrenched up. His fingers bent at wrong angles and reached out.

"What the fu—!" I backed up as my shock turned to terror.

Jace grabbed my shoulders and pushed me to the side. I stumbled to my feet, barely gaining purchase to keep from falling on my face.

"Get back!" Jace cried.

I couldn't rip my gaze away until Jace moved in front of me, breaking my line of sight.

"How was he moving? How is that possible, shouldn't he be dead with that many injuries?"

Jace didn't answer as he continued to force me off our path. "Ray, hurry. He's up."

I looked behind and tripped. Jace caught me, barely managing to keep me upright. The man who'd been so still had already pulled himself to his feet. And he was running, closing the distance between us faster than should have been possible.

"We need to find somewhere to hide," Jace said between breaths.

Clumsy footsteps pounded against the pavement after us as we ran past several boarded up shops. Up ahead, a store with a broken window promised some semblance of shelter. I pushed my body to its limit. Long past the burning stage, and I could feel my muscles straining to keep up with my demands.

My bag bounced, threatening to knock me off balance. I wanted to throw it away, to get rid of the extra weight and awkward sway, but the cure was inside.

We jumped through the window, over the shards of glass that were still stuck in the frame, skidding to a stop. I took in what we had to work with—isles and isles of craft supplies. Some shelves were knocked over, scattering items across the floor.

I clenched my jaw, wishing we'd stumbled into a sporting goods store instead. *What am I going to do, macramé him to death?* I thought bitterly.

"Jace, we need to find something to use as weapons," I said, gripping onto his hand.

I ran down the isles with Jace in tow. We stopped by the tiny bottles of paint. I grabbed as many as I could, cradling them in my arms as I moved through the store.

Glass skittered across the floor as a small display near the front fell and crashed to the ground. I cried out, but Jace clamped his hand over my mouth to stop the noise from escaping.

I was thankful for his foresight of how I'd react. It bothered me I'd become one of those girls, the ones who shrieked at every unexpected thing. My brain struggled to focus through the fog of endless exhaustion. All I wanted to do was sleep.

Slowly, Jace peeked around the shelf. He drew back with sharp, stilted movements, pushing me even further behind him.

My stomach tightened into knots, the anticipation killing me. I nearly choked on the tension that enveloped us. Every step that man took as he moved about searching for us—*hunting for us*—created a ripple in the air that crawled along my skin like a million spiders. I held myself as still as possible, trying not to giveaway our position.

I swallowed, the sound almost deafening to my ears in the unnatural silence. My throat contracted as a tickle worked its way up. Then, a cough forced its way free. I tried to stop it.

My hand shot up, but it was too late, the paint I clutched to my chest slowed my movements. It came out a strangled sound of half-cough half-grunt, only making it worse. I covered my mouth at the same time as the paint fell to the ground. Each bounce of the plastic bottles against the tile floor made an ear-shattering thump.

The half-second of silence that followed seemed to last a lifetime. Of course, the deafening silence didn't last long enough…

Chapter Twenty-Two

Run, Run, Run

A bone-chilling growl dripping with rabid hunger sliced through the air as pounding footsteps charged, growing closer impossibly fast.

Jace kicked a small side shelf filled with glass jars. They landed with a crash, sending a rainbow of beads and glass flying.

The man, once my hero, slid and fell, but he managed to right himself inhumanly fast, the beads underfoot hardly slowed his pace.

Fresh blood dribbled down the man's chin and clung to the scruff of his face.

His eyes locked on me, and I could have sworn he'd recognized me. He kept moving forward, determined to reach me and —

"Raylinn!" Jace said harshly as he tugged on my arm.

I still clutched the bottles of paint, wondering what I had planned to do with them in the first place. My mind was sluggish; I couldn't focus. I took a step toward Jace as he tried to clear a path through a myriad of craft supplies strewn about the floor.

Blinding pain shot through my head. I blinked… and then I was staring up at the ceiling. I tried to move, tried to stand, but the scruffy man was nearly on top of me. The only things within reach were the small bottles of paint I'd been holding. I took a bottle in each hand, flipped the tops open, aimed and squeezed.

He lunged at me as ribbons of red and blue splattered across his face. I rolled and he landed, temporarily blinded, on the spot where I had been.

Jace gripped my arm, pulling me up.

My head still pounded, but I let Jace lead me between knocked over displays. I looked over my shoulder.

"Jace," I choked out, "he's coming back."

I should have helped the man who had saved me. I never should have left him there. He'd been badly hurt, and his blood still dripped from his clothing. Shock had to be the only reason he was able to be this active. He was letting his virus-induced insanity rule his rage over my callousness.

A large knitting needle flew past my face as I turned to run again. Then another. And another. The first one hit the man in the right shoulder, jerking it backwards, but it still didn't slow him down. The next one missed.

The third hit the center of his chest, directly into his heart.

Half of his body slumped as he fell to the ground, his knees making a hard cracking sound against the tiled floor. Still, he continued his pursuit, dragging his body. I gagged and turned away, following closely behind Jace.

It wasn't natural. It wasn't right. Even in shock, he shouldn't have been able to continue. *Jace had hit his heart.*

As soon as our feet hit the pavement outside, we ran full speed. We didn't look back. My only thought was to create as much distance as possible between us and the craft store.

We didn't pause until we made it halfway through the next barricade. I collapsed to my hands and knees on a grassy lawn as I sucked in deep, gasping breaths.

"Jace, what the hell was that? How is that possible?" I tilted my head, squinting up at his face. The bright morning sun was nearly blinding as it silhouetted his body.

"We can't stop here," Jace said lifting me up by the arm.

I jerked away.

"Tell me," I demanded. "Why was he like that?"

Even though I knew it wasn't a good place to stop, I still felt compelled to know what was happening. These people weren't acting right, they weren't acting... *human*. Insanity wasn't like this; this was different—something out of a horror movie.

He closed his eyes for a moment and pinched his nose before meeting my gaze again, his mouth set in a hard line as if he were having an inner debate.

"The virus will cause a metabolic state that mimics death as it attacks the nervous system and takes control. It feeds on parts of the brain, causing it to lose the ability to think rationally—as you and I do—and the body is left with nothing but the basic instincts of hunting and aggression."

The tone in his voice made me think there was more to the story than what he was telling me. He sounded like he'd been there. But that was impossible.

"It was terrible. The fear alone was enough to cause wide spread panic. The symptoms effected people in two ways: similar to the man who chased us, or a long painful death."

"You told me it happened centuries ago."

"It was…" Jace trailed off.

"How can you talk like you lived through it then?" I whispered. My mind whirled. It wasn't possible, it didn't add up.

Jace averted his eyes. "I was in one of the last cities to become infected. I was already in stasis for over half of the required term by the time it reached my city."

"That would make you—" My eyes shot up to meet his, and my words came out hoarse. There was no way he could be that old… "Hundreds of years old."

"Just over seven hundred years—using your calendar." The slightest blush colored his face. "But I've spent almost all of that time in a stasis chamber."

I opened my mouth to speak, but closed it once I saw his shift in demeanor. Jace lifted his chin and scanned the area. I followed his line of sight. I didn't see anything to worry over, but with how much things had changed, that meant nothing.

Red clouds reached up toward the sky from various spots

in the city. There was no rhyme or reason to it. The faint smell of burning wood drifted on the soft spring breeze. I wondered if the fires were from looters, or if they were from something a lot darker than that.

"Please, Ray," he said, using the shortened version of my name for the first time in a while. It sounded weird hearing it from him after all this time, but nevertheless, it was welcome. "We need to get moving again. We can talk about it on the way if you want, but the virus seems to be infecting at a faster rate than it was a few days ago."

Those last few words snapped my mind back to why we were crossing the city. *Toby.*

"No, let's go," I said. I adjusted the bag over my shoulder and started jogging along with Jace, quickly speeding up into a full on run.

Only a few blocks away from Miranda's, I took the lead, skirting around my own sector to save time. I was growing more and more exhausted as the day went on. My lungs burned and a tiredness, which had nothing to do with the amount of running I had done, enveloped me. It was as if my will to move became more and more listless as the sun trekked across the sky. When I found myself jogging slower than a walk, I switched to one.

Jace followed behind, allowing me to set the pace, never once pushing me past my limits. I don't know if he was giving himself space to avoid talking about his past, or if he was also grateful for the break in pace.

Each time I turned my head to look back, he avoided my eyes, staring off into the distance instead. I let our earlier conversation drop completely. In the end, the details didn't matter. I'd only been using it as a distraction anyway.

The sun set as we crossed the final highway separating us from our goal. About a quarter of a mile away, I could see the iron fence that was built along the road beneath the bridge ahead. I paused next to a large bush that grew along the side of the road, using it for cover.

Men with large guns stood on the bridge above, pacing the width of the road below as their eyes scanned either side for anyone stupid enough to try climbing over it, even with the barbed wire spread thickly across the top.

I squinted into the distance. A crowd of people walked toward the fence. Sentinels on all sides, herded them like cattle. Nausea rolled through me at the sight.

"Ray," Jace pulled my attention away from the scene we were trying to avoid. He squeezed my knee.

"Sorry," I mumbled, following him away from the crowds and soldiers.

What was wrong with me? I couldn't focus on the task at hand. We'd left with one objective, and I couldn't keep it in my mind. It was as if a fog had slowly rolled in and obscured my thoughts until I was turned around, utterly lost and confused. Kept only on track by the automatic determination of my feet against the pavement, and Jace's guiding hands.

My eyes began to droop, and I blinked at a large brick and stone house across the street. We'd made it. I took a step forward, wanting nothing more than to finally give my brother the cure.

Jace grabbed my hand and pulled me back into the shadows of a bush lining the neighboring yard. I grunted in surprise, but then spotted the reason for his abrupt movements.

A large tank rolled around the corner and headed down the street. A spotlight swung from side to side, sweeping the area. We moved back until we were completely hidden. We waited, crouched against branches and leaves. Jace's hand rested on my upper arm, and I realized I was leaning on him, barely managing to keep upright.

After the tank passed, we waited a minute before standing. Jace held my hand and didn't let go until we entered my friend's house.

The lights were off, and we didn't dare turn them on. I walked blindly, counting on my memory from all the years I'd spent in this house.

My foot caught on a rug, and I felt my body lurch forward. My shin hit something sharp and wooden, but I landed on a soft form.

I quickly scrambled back, expecting whoever I'd landed on to curse me for my inability to stay on my feet. But no words came. I placed my hands on the floor to push myself up, but they slipped on a cool tacky substance.

I froze. Small tremors worked their way through my limbs, shaking my entire body.

"Jace…" I whispered. "Jace, help me up. Jace!" Panic tore its way through my voice.

His strong hands lifted me and pressed me to his chest.

"Oh my God, Jace. Is this —" I couldn't finish. The scent of copper filled my nose.

He didn't answer but made soft shushing noises as he rubbed my back. After I found my legs and could finally breathe again, he guided me to the kitchen sink in the other room. Jace slowly lowered me to the floor while he searched for a hand towel, wetting it before kneeling at my side.

I stared at the dark substance on my hands. Jace set to cleaning the blood off me as best he could. I watched his meticulous motions. It was like watching a scene outside of myself. It didn't feel real.

My head lulled to the side. The yellow light from a street lamp came through the window as it flickered to life.

I turned away, and my gaze fell on a sheet of paper on the floor, half under the stove to my left. I slipped my hand out of Jace's. At some point, he'd taken it and I hadn't noticed. I stood and went to pick up the paper, pausing as I straightened when a wave of dizziness turned the world on end, but it passed as fast as it had come on.

Squinting, I brought it close to my face, trying to make out the words. I was surprised to see my dad's handwriting. It was messy, unlike his usual perfect script.

Ray, we had to leave. They found us. They are coming for —

The note ended there. The R trailed off in a scribble as if he'd been interrupted.

No! We were here, with the cure, they couldn't have taken my family! "Jace, they aren't here…"

It never occurred to me that the form I fell on could be one of my family members. I shoved the note into his hands, rushed back to the other room, and flipped the light on, not caring if someone outside saw.

Broken furniture was strewn about, and in the path of the doorway was Miranda's father. I quickly scanned the rest of the room; the only other body was her mother. Blood oozed from various spots in their backs. Whatever had happened, it had been recent.

My family was nowhere to be seen, and I was grateful for it. Tears welled up in my eyes as my heart broke for the people who'd always been a second set of parents, and for my best friend.

Pressure built in my head, causing it to pound mercilessly.

I couldn't breathe. The walls were closing in on me. The edges of my vision blurred and darkened.

Then everything went black.

CHAPTER TWENTY-THREE

After it All

I opened my eyes and blinked. My tongue darted out between parched lips as I tried to focus my vision. Pale pink light streaming in from the window made the room glow. The hard tiles of the floor sent a cold ache through my body. My joints were stiff as I shifted, and my muscles protested every movement. Jace's arm fell from around me as I sat up and looked around.

Miranda's kitchen? I pressed a cool hand to my forehead, trying to shake the haziness from my mind. Jace groaned next to me, shifting.

The synapses in my brain tried to fire, attempting to remember why I was here, but merely sparked before fading. The constant pounding of a hammer rattled inside my skull with every beat of my heart, as it painfully pumped away, unconcerned with my current predicament.

"What happened?" I asked as quietly as I could through the desert in my throat.

"I must have fallen asleep, I'm sorry." Jace rubbed his hands over his face as he straightened. His shoulders slumped.

The chirping of birds outside was like nails on a chalkboard to my nerves. Then the realization dawned on me. "Why are we still here? We have to get the cure to Toby."

My heart thumped in my throat. I had no idea how much time my brother had before he would succumb to the virus completely. I wanted to blame Jace for letting me sleep, though I knew it wasn't his fault. The only thing left for me to do was to get up and go find my brother.

I must have had a scowl on my face because he said, "Raylinn, you hit your head when you fainted, I couldn't get you to wake up."

I forced the muscles of my face to relax.

"I fainted?" I asked. Then, slowly, the memories of the night before came back to me. *Darkness. Tripping. Blood... so much blood. Miranda's parents.* My stomach rolled.

Reaching up, I grabbed the counter and pulled myself up, shaking out the pins and needles that had settled in my legs. I'd slept all night. Precious hours that I needed—that Toby needed—were gone. The overwhelming desire to lay back down on the unforgiving floor and sleep for a year still invaded every fiber of my being.

But I refused to let my exhaustion win.

Find Toby. Give him the maybe *cure. Then I can sleep.*

I picked up my bag from the floor and slung it over my shoulder.

"It's not too late, Ray," Jace said softly, his hand cupped my face. His eyes were full of sympathy and strength.

It was then that I realized we'd been dragging each other back and forth across town for days, never once able to slow down. His presence by my side was always a constant source of comfort and safety. If it weren't for him, I never would have made it. I would've given up, or at the very least, been taken over by the virus.

The moment we met, he'd saved me. From a life of settling, of playing things safe, from placing my heart in an iron box never to feel what I felt with him. And he continued to save me from the dangers that threatened the world.

I nodded. "Let's keep going."

We left through the sliding glass door in the kitchen. Smoke filled the air, making everything hazy. I wondered how out of control the fires we saw had become.

Traveling during the day wasn't ideal, not with tanks patrolling the area, not with areas of highway blocked off, and not with soldiers leading large groups of people to whatever they had in store for them. It was hard enough for Jace and me to make it anywhere, being pushed around with who knows how many others seemed terrifying.

I swore under my breath. I turned to Jace. "I don't know where they went. They never said in the note."

"After you passed out, I studied the note. I knew you would have wanted me to." He looked at me sheepishly. "I was hoping there would be an obvious clue as to where they were headed, but there wasn't."

"No, this can't be happening," I gripped my hair with my hands and tugged at the roots. I could feel hot tears prickling the backs of my eyes. "We were so close."

"The last word was interrupted. At first, I didn't think anything of it. Now I'm wondering if your authorities were the reason it was never finished."

"No, no, no, no, no," I croaked out through emotions thick enough to strangle. I blinked and tears slid down my face. All that running, all that searching… it had been for nothing.

"That's good news, don't you see?"

I looked at him, my mouth hung open. "How is that good news?"

"Because it tells us where to look. Remember the soldiers we saw yesterday guarding the people under the bridge? If your family was taken…" He trailed off, letting the dots connect themselves in my brain.

"Then it's likely they will be in a group like that." I wiped my face with dirty hands.

"We just have to stay in the bushes and hide until we find

them. We'll move slowly, but we can still move faster than the crowd."

Going through alleys and backyards, we made it to the highway around noon. Unfortunately, the route we took there to avoid the military was still half a mile from the first gated area. Even from my limited vantage point, I could see there were dozens of people confined to that tiny space, being funneled through to the next gated area.

The open area between was only a few blocks, but it might as well have been several miles. While crossing it, they would be vulnerable to the runners.

Abandoned cars sat along the sides of the road, and some in the middle. A thin layer of dust had already settled. I was just glad whatever made people abandoned their cars hadn't happened during rush hour, or it would have been impossible to cross with the bumper-to-bumper traffic.

Jace used his height to see through the thinning top of a bush we had clung to for cover.

"Stay low, and don't move fast if you can help it," he whispered. "Go, now."

I opened my mouth to ask if he was coming with me, but quickly snapped it shut. *Toby.*

Heart pounding in my chest, I crouched low. Heat rose from

the asphalt and instantly, sweat broke out across my forehead. I wove between the cars, trying to avoid touching their metal frames.

Crossing was easier than I'd expected, though it made sense the majority of the authorities would be focusing on the group of people within, not looking for people sneaking around. So as long as we didn't stand out, we'd be fine.

The brush grew thinner as we approached the bridge. A cement wall about the height of a car ran along the side of the road. It would be perfect cover, but we had to make it through the open gap first. If we'd had the cover of night, we could have used it to go in to find my family, then get out with them.

It would prove to be more difficult in daylight, but I hoped it wasn't impossible.

I looked to Jace, who nodded but waited for me to make the move.

Men along the top of the bridge were looking over to make sure no one was trying to leave the group. They would move, then stop, then repeat the process, never taking their eyes off the group for long. More men on the ground rounded up the back. Their eyes locked on the crowd with their guns poised.

Slipping my hand into Jace's, we waited. The second the men above moved, I raced forward.

Something pinged against the ground. Dirt flew up in my face in a small explosion. I stopped in my tracks, jerking Jace to a halt as well. Another ping sent a shower of dirt spraying me.

I turned away, only to have another spray of dirt scatter around me.

Someone was shooting at us. My feet cemented to the ground, and I stopped trying to move forward.

"Stop," a man's voice commanded.

Jace made a slight movement, which stole my attention. "Don't move," I warned quietly.

I looked to the man. He was on the ground, but had been out of my sight when I had looked. I cursed myself for not being more careful.

I wanted to tell Jace to run and hide. I had no idea what this camouflaged man would do if he knew Jace wasn't human, but it was too late to warn him, the man was too close.

"What are you two doing outside the gate?" he demanded. He planted his boots firmly in the gravel, taking a wide, intimidating stance. The man's fingers gripped his riffle across his chest and his glare fixed in on me, daring me to run so he could use it.

"Uh, we," I started but was cut off before I could finish.

"Get back inside! Now!" he ordered with a jerk of his head.

I nodded vigorously. The man spat at our feet and narrowed his eyes. Without waiting for him to say anymore, I pulled Jace past him with quick steps. He let me drag him until we were in the thick of the crowd, then stopped abruptly. I looked over my shoulder to see him frowning at me.

"Raylinn, I need to rest," he said.

He looked worn. His cheeks slightly hollowed, more than

what looked healthy. It stole the strength his features had held when I'd seen him the day he first stepped foot off his ship. Jace's skin held a pallor that made me worry.

"Okay," I agreed. To be honest, I'd wanted to rest as well. My breathing was labored from the day's walk. Each pull of my breath had turned to agony.

A siren sounded, low and drawn out in its mournful cry. The eerie noise reminded me of the ones used during the cold war.

Before I could figure out what was happening, we were herded like cattle between two gates that crossed the now deserted highway. It looked like an earthquake had hit. Large chunks of concrete had fallen from various places. A month of disuse had allowed vines to grow up the sides. It made the city feel wild and foreign to this world.

I looked up at the sentinels in their box above us. This was wrong; this was too dangerous. No one ever knew how close the runners were. They were fast and too quiet to be noticed in a crowd this large and loud. We should have crossed in small groups. People were talking, crying, fighting... The noise would call to them. Then we would all be lost.

My heart pounded wildly in my chest as I choked on the adrenaline of panic.

I looked up to see a man on the bridge wave his hand in a quick circle a few times, then pointed north. The gate started to open, buzzing in warning. The red light flashed before the gates swung open. People shoved, forcing me along with the riptide of bodies. The main body of or group slowed as we made it to the intersection beneath the bridge. A few continued to run, but many slowed to a walk.

People shoved their way past. I cried out as a meaty hand landed on my upper chest, pushing me back. My hand slipped from Jace's. I would have fallen to the ground if there hadn't been countless others there pushing me in the opposite direction. I could see the distance between Jace and I growing.

I lunged forward, refusing to let the panicked crowd drag me from him.

"Raylinn!"

I heard my name shouted out from behind, but I ignored it. I forced my way through the never ceasing crowd to the edges, standing on tiptoes looking. Jace was pushing his way into the crowd, but there were too many. His progress was slow. I tried to weave through the masses, but for every step I took, the crowd forced me back two.

"Jace!" I called his name.

"Ray?" My dad's voice caught my attention. I spun around, ricocheting off people like a pinball as they passed.

"Dad?" I called out. Jace reached me just before my parents. My mom's eyes were red and puffy. "Dad, what's going on?" I asked. "Where's Toby? Miranda?"

He shook his head. "She didn't make it."

"Your brother tried to run." My mom grabbed at my sleeves, her eyes wide with the horror of reliving the moment over again as she told me. "They caught him, Ray. They shot him right there in the street!"

Tears fell down her cheeks and I pulled her in for a tight hug, letting her sob into my shoulder. My blood seemed to freeze in my veins. I'd had the cure, I'd found my family, but it hadn't been enough to save Toby. I wanted to smash the cure, I wanted to wail and scream. I wanted to break everything. Most of all, I wanted to take my anger out on the idiots who had killed my brother in cold blood before I'd had the chance to save him.

But I didn't move. My face remained a mask of cold stone.

"They're moving us to the northern sectors," my father said.

"What?" My jaw dropped. "No, they can't, there are infected people there, it's worse than we thought."

The gate to the north screeched. Metal ground against metal, rattling as it shifted.

A voice crackled over loud speakers above the sea of people. "Everyone walk through to the next sector in a calm and organized fashion."

I wanted to smack the man who said that. "Calm and organized?" I snorted.

My anger vanished as a blood-curdling scream cleaved the air. And for a second, the mass of bodies seemed to hold its collective breath.

"Runners!"

The following second, the force of too many people pushed against us. Still holding onto my mother, we fell, pulling apart as we hit the ground. Jace was quick to lift me up as Dad helped Mom to her feet. She grasped at her left arm.

Gunshots rained down around us.

"Jace, get her out of here. Take her somewhere safe. We'll find you two later," Dad ordered.

"What? No!" I couldn't believe my ears. I didn't want to leave them when we'd only just found them again.

"Protect her," he said before turning to me. "I love you."

Jace dragged me away. I tried to fight it, but the mass of people wasn't slowing, and it helped pull me from my family. I kept my eyes on the two people who meant more to me than I could say. The last of my family was being swallowed by the crowd.

A pale, sickly hand latched on to Dad's shoulder and jerked him around, breaking our eye contact. The large maw opened wide and bit down. My mother screamed, but was lost as another runner pushed her to the ground.

I clawed at Jace's hands. I couldn't leave them, I couldn't let the horrible fate I knew awaited, happen. I could give them the cure! Reaching into my bag, I grabbed at the glass vile. I jerked my hand back. Small shards of glass imbedded into my hand, stained with the blue cure. It must have broken when I fell in the craft store. A sob tore its way free from my throat.

"There's nothing you can do," Jace said, his voice stern, but sympathetic. He had also lost his family. I turned and ran with him toward the opening that would take us away from the stampede, and the infected.

It took more energy than I could spare to get clear, but we finally made it to the edge of the crowd.

A hand grabbed my upper arm and twisted. I cried out and fell to my knees. Then the hand released me, and I was free. I looked up and Jace stood behind the man's fallen form. He lowered his hand, sparks of energy still dancing on his palm.

Jace helped me to my feet. My legs threatened to buckle from under me as I stood. We ran until we were far from the highway, far from the uniforms, and far from everyone I knew.

Chapter Twenty-Four

In the End

When we finally stopped running, we were in the old, run-down industrial area. I tried to catch my breath, but a coughing fit shook my body. I doubled over from the force of it. I wiped at my mouth and looked at the smear of red across my skin.

I looked behind to see if we were being followed. Nothing but empty streets stretched out for miles. Smoke filled the sky, turning it a sickly orange. As if the world were on fire trying to cleanse itself of the disaster, which had spread without mercy.

Jace tried to comfort me, but I pushed away, keeping my head down. I rubbed the blood off on my jeans and continued up the hill toward an abandoned factory of some kind. Jace walked at my side, shoulders slumped. Much like me, his gaze was on the ground, only seeing where his next step would fall.

In the shelter of a rusted building, we collapsed against a wall. It felt good to sit, not having to run, and just being able to breathe.

"Raylinn, you're sick," Jace said.

"No, I'm fine," I denied.

He lifted a hand, and his thumb brushed against my bottom lip, coming away with blood. "Don't be stubborn, Ray. We can't get the cure to your brother, but you can still take it."

"I can't, Jace." I looked down at my hand, and started plucking the tiny shards of glass out the best I could.

Jace grabbed my wrist and brought my hand to his face. He looked at the cut, then at me in horror. Dropping his hold, he grabbed the bag and dumped it upside-down. Fragments of blue-coated glass sprinkled around the last of my food bars. The thick syrup was everywhere.

Jace and I had lost everyone we'd ever known, and now we were alone in this strange new world. *This dying world.*

Screams from down the hill still echoed through the city, slowly growing fewer and fewer as the sun began to set. I didn't want to think about why.

A sob ripped its way up my throat. "I don't want to be one of those... those... things."

Jace gathered me in his arms. "You won't."

I tried to push away, not wanting to infect him as well.

"You don't know that," I said between unsteady breaths.

"The strain you have is slower than what that man had," he explained.

I started coughing again. This time, managing to push away.

"Ray—"

"No, you can't. I don't want you to get this too."

There was a heavy silence between us before he answered. "I already have it. I was so focused on keeping you safe that I didn't realize it at first." He hesitated for a second. "I am afraid I am the reason you have it."

I stared blankly at him, trying to understand his words. Jace looked at me expectantly, as if he thought I'd be angry with him. But I wasn't.

I dropped my head against the metal wall and looked up, trying to blink my tears away. "I would have ended up sick anyway. I was never going to be the only one to escape this. I wouldn't want to be the only one left," I said.

Warm amber eyes studied my face. I tried to memorize every last detail of his features, imposing the memory I had of him on top of the worn down version.

The sun finally set and we were left in a world of darkness. Jace cleared away the remains of my bag and the food covered in glass shards. He put his arm around me, and I rested my head on his shoulder. Tears fell silently down my cheeks as I cried over our fate..

My heart and mind were numb. I didn't want this fate, but I didn't want to be alone in the world either.

We tried our best to sleep. It should have been easy with the exhaustion I knew we both felt. Maybe it was the threat of the end approaching at the speed of a train, or maybe it was the pain in our lungs. It didn't matter. I savored every second of his touch. The way his breath moved strands of my hair across my forehead, the feeling of his heart beating against my cheek, the caress of his fingertips along my arm.

Screams went on throughout the night, until silence was all that was left.

Dawn slowly crept up. The fingers of light wove their way through the twilight of morning chasing the full moon below the horizon to make way for another nightmarish day.

I couldn't help but think about how it had all started.

A desire for world peace approached with fear, Jace and his people looking for home.

It was inevitable.

It didn't matter what Thral'el or Doctor Lar'ruk were up to. It was entirely possible our people were never meant to live together. After all, it was the combination that had mutated the virus, turning it into this unpredictable and inescapable force.

This was it.

War was ending forever.

The earth plagued by bloodshed throughout all of human history was finally finding peace that had cost more than anyone could have bargained for. It was a long and painful journey, but it was finally being achieved. Just not how we had expected.

The last sounds anyone heard were bone-shattering screams—screams from the pain of the virus taking over, or from being eaten alive by the infected runners. It was enough to stop a heart from beating if it hadn't been from their own mouths. The virus burned through their veins, stripping away the last of their humanity.

I pulled away from Jace to sit up straight. I stared into amber eyes that drowned out the drab, grey cement ceiling that sheltered us. I would have loved to see the sky one last time, but even that was an impossible wish. Fire and smoke turned the sky brown and hazy, blocking the sun's rays. Smoke wafted in from outside and filled our space, burning my nostrils.

I could feel him stiffen. The muscles of his jaw clenched, and I could tell he was in pain as well.

I heard my lungs rasping through my ears as fire raced through my nerves.

I wouldn't scream. He was being strong for me, so I would be strong for him.

Jace wrapped his long fingers around my hand to provide what little comfort he could, as his arm pulled me against his chest.

Jace said nothing. After all, what could he have said that would right anything? Words would have been meaningless, but the emotion he felt shone through.

Love was an emotion alien to him. He'd told me as much when we'd first met. I wanted to laugh at that; something alien to an alien.

Throughout the night, the occasional distant scream echoed all around us, sending shivers through me with every mournful cry.

Over the next several days, they died out, one by one, growing farther apart.

On the third day, we sat holding each other, when all that was left was the short heaviness of my breathing, and the slowing of my heart beat. I could feel myself fading in and out.

Soon, the howling wind would be the only sound to greet the world, wearing down the buildings crumbling under the weight of age.

The distant screams faded out and the world for the first time in history was silently peaceful.

We'd woken up in the factory, to the sun streaming in through the broken window. I took a deep breath and let it out slowly, taking a mental check of my body. I felt… *refreshed*. All symptoms of the virus had vanished. Somehow, we'd survived. We didn't die, and we hadn't become runners.

I rubbed the sleep from my eyes.

"Why didn't we die?" I asked as I sat up. The pain in my lungs, the cough, and the rawness of my throat had vanished as if I'd never been sick.

"I don't know. We didn't have access to the cure." His eyes traveled to the remains of the broken vile. He brushed a hand against my forehead. "How do you feel?"

"I feel fine," I muttered, still trying to understand.

I sat back against the cold, metal wall and chewed my thumbnail. Why had we been spared when no one else had?

I thought back to everything that had happened. The only thing that set Jace and me apart was the fact that we were together. What had the doctor's notes said? *No cure, it didn't bond.*

I wondered if the answer could lie within those four short words. I rolled them around my mind, over and over and over.

After a while, a thought occurred to me. "Jace, remember when we were going through the doctor's notes, you said there wasn't a cure because it didn't bond."

Jace frowned. "Yes, I remember that."

"What if it meant something else? Lar'ruk mentioned something about a bond between us when he was dragging me to his lab. What if it wasn't the chemical bond, but a bond between... *us.*"

He looked thoughtful for a long moment. "That would make sense. What we have, is considered a bond on my planet."

"If we survived because of a bond, maybe there are others out there who've bonded too."

"I don't know, Raylinn." He said quirking an eyebrow.

"I think it's likely, on a planet this large, there has to be others. Besides, it's not like we have anything better to do with our time now."

It didn't take much after that to get him to agree. Maybe he saw that I needed a purpose, maybe he'd felt it too.

Hope.

Hope that we weren't alone. That not everything in this world had died.

Carefully, we made our way back toward town. It was silent. Void of all the noises you find in a city—the sounds of birds chirping, cars, people—is all absent.

The closer we got to town, the more time I spent with my eyes on the horizon, only glancing down to avoid the bodies we came across. Many were victims, but just as many were the runners, their greenish hue setting them apart.

I supposed whatever had fueled them had finally run out, but it didn't make them any more pleasant to look at. After searching the city for days, we knew we were the only ones left.

Armed with baseball bats we'd found in a sports store, we spent three full days wandering the city, calling out to anyone. My throat was hoarse by the time we finished, a good hoarse though, from yelling and not the pain of the virus ripping its way through my veins.

We returned to the factory on the hill. It felt safest there, more peaceful far away from the destruction. I could pretend the city was sleeping.

Over a dinner of cold canned beans, we discussed our plan. We'd stayed one last night before heading out in search of others.

It wasn't much of a plan, mainly zigzagging up and down the country looking for survivors.

An hour before the sun came up, I woke, unable to sleep any longer. I was anxious to start our journey.

Jace slept soundly on the dusty cement floor next to me. Quietly, I slipped out from under the blanket we shared, and made my way to the crest of the hill.

I wrapped my arms around myself to ward off the chill of the night air. I scanned the horizon, admiring the beautiful lush valley that once nestled my home.

Epilogue

Sound of Silence

They say be careful what you wish for, it might just come true.

Everyone wished for world peace. But now, as I stand here, silence engulfs me. This isn't what anyone had in mind or wanted, but now, the world is at peace. With so many ideas and beliefs, everything that made us wonderfully different from each other, we were never a species capable of pure peace, and the world could never have achieved it so long as we were around.

Peace didn't mean what everyone had assumed. It never meant everyone getting along regardless of who we were. Something would have to give—the very thing that made us unique individuals, or life.

I look at the skyline. The red-stained sky has cleared as the fires die out. My home, my city, is all but destroyed. It has been ransacked, boarded up, and burned to the ground.

"Raylinn?" Jace asks as he walks up to my side, taking my hand in his. I lift my gaze to meet his warm amber eyes. "Are you ready to go now?"

I look back to the city one last time and take in a deep, shuttering breath before turning my back on it.

"Yes," I say. Slinging my bag over my shoulder, we walk down the hill toward the edge of the city.

We will go south, then east. We don't have any destination in mind, not yet. But it doesn't matter how long it will take, we'll spend the rest of our lives searching for others like us, guided only by hope. With any luck, we aren't the only ones left on this now silent planet.

ACKNOWLEDGMENTS

This book, like all books, came with its own unique set of challenges. I was blessed enough to be surrounded by wonderful people who were not only pillars of support but rather so much more than words can say.

Sometimes the world can throw you a curveball that just takes all the air out of your lungs and threatens to take you out of the game. But having people around who love and support you can be the one thing that saves you from falling down.

My editor Kristine for working me through everything life threw at me. Your flexibility and skill saved me so much stress.

Mom and Dad, words can't even describe how much your continued support means to me. You believed not just in me, but in my dreams.

I don't know what I would have done without my sprint buddies, Konstanz and Erin. When the worst head cold threatened to drain all creativity from me for life, it was because of you that I was able to start again and fight through the fog.

Audrey, thank you for your support and encouragement and going through this insane process with me. I can't imagine this journey without you. It certainly wouldn't have been half as fun.

Lastly, thank you to my husband for helping me find space to focus and telling me to sit my butt back down and get back to writing.

ABOUT THE AUTHOR

Ali Winters is the USA TODAY Bestselling author of several series filled with romance, magic, and adventure.

Her first love will always be fantasy, but she fully admits to being obsessed with coffee and T-Rex, and has a weakness for love interests that walk the line between gray and villainy.

Ali was born and raised in the PNW but now currently resides in the wastelands that time forgot, with impossibly cold winters, and summers that are too short. She spends her days with her husband and alpha of her two dog pack. (They have assimilated her as one of their own and since she's the only one with opposable thumbs, have made her their leader.)

When she's not consumed with creating magical worlds for readers to get lost in, she can be found walking, reading, designing graphics, and creating art in various mediums.

Visit Ali on the web at www.aliwinters.com
Facebook.com/authoraliwinters
instagram.com/authoraliwinters

To subscribe to Ali's monthly newsletter for new releases, exclusive sneak peeks, and visit
www.aliwinters.com/newsletter

9 781945 238048